JEANETTE WINTERSON

Jeanette Winterson CBE was born in Manchester. Adopted by Pentecostal parents she was raised to be a missionary. This did and didn't work out.

Discovering early the power of books, she left home at sixteen to live in a Mini and get on with her education. After graduating from Oxford University she worked for a while in the theatre and published her first novel at twenty-five. *Oranges Are Not The Only Fruit* is based on her own upbringing but using herself as a fictional character. She scripted the novel into a BAFTA-winning BBC drama. Twenty-seven years later she re-visited that material in the bestselling memoir *Why Be Happy When You Could Be Normal?* She has written ten novels for adults, and her most recent work, *Frankissstein* was longlisted for the Booker Prize 2019. Jeanette has also written children's books, non-fiction and screenplays. She is Professor of New Writing at the University of Manchester. She lives in the Cotswolds in a wood and in Spitalfields, London.

She believes that art is for everyone and it is her mission to prove it.

ALSO BY JEANETTE WINTERSON

NOVELS

Oranges Are Not The
Only Fruit
The Passion
Sexing the Cherry
Written on the Body
Art & Lies
Gut Symmetries
The Powerbook
Lighthousekeeping
The Stone Gods
The Gap of Time

SHORT STORIES

The World and Other
Places
Midsummer Nights (ed.)
Christmas Days

NOVELLAS

Weight (Myth)
The Daylight Gate
(Horror)

NON-FICTION

Art Objects: Essays in
Ecstasy and Effrontery
Why Be Happy When
You Could Be Normal?
Courage Calls to Courage
Everywhere

COLLABORATIONS

Land (with Antony
Gormley and Clare
Richardson)

CHILDREN'S BOOKS

Tanglewreck
The Lion, the Unicorn
and Me
The King of Capri
The Battle of the Sun

COMIC BOOKS

Boating for Beginners

JEANETTE WINTERSON

FRAN KISS STEIN

A LOVE STORY

VINTAGE

1 3 5 7 9 10 8 6 4 2

Vintage
20 Vauxhall Bridge Road,
London SW1V 2SA

Vintage is part of the Penguin Random House group of companies
whose addresses can be found at global.penguinrandomhouse.com.

Penguin
Random House
UK

First published by Jonathan Cape in 2019
First published by Vintage in 2020

penguin.co.uk/vintage

A CIP catalogue record for this book is available from the
British Library

ISBN 9781784709952

Printed and bound in Great Britain by Clays Ltd, Elcograf S.p.A.

Penguin Random House is committed to a sustainable future for our
business, our readers and our planet. This book is made from Forest
Stewardship Council® certified paper.

We may lose and we may win though we will never be here again.

Eagles, 'Take It Easy'

Lake Geneva, 1816

Reality is water-soluble.

What we could see, the rocks, the shore, the trees, the
boats on the lake, had lost their usual definition and
blurred into the long grey of a week's rain. Even the
house, that we fancied was made of stone, wavered inside
a heavy mist and through that mist, sometimes, a door
or a window appeared like an image in a dream.

Every solid thing had dissolved into its watery
equivalent.

Our clothes did not dry. When we came in, and we must
come in, because we must go out, we brought the
weather with us. Waterlogged leather. Wool that stank
of sheep.

There is mould on my underclothes.

This morning I had the idea to walk naked. What is the
use of sodden cloth? Of covered buttons so swollen in
their buttonholes that I had to be cut out of my
dress yesterday?

1

This morning my bed was as wet as if I had sweated all night. The windows were misty with my own breath. Where the fire burned in the grate the wood hissed like a dejection of nature. I left you sleeping and I trod silently down the filmy stairs, my feet wet.

Naked.

I opened the main door to the house. The rain continued, steady and indifferent. For seven days now it had fallen, not faster, not slower, not increasing, not abating. The earth could swallow no more and the ground everywhere was spongy – the gravel paths oozed water, and several springs had burst through the orderly garden, eroding soil that deposited itself in thick black puddles at our gate.

But this morning it was behind the house I went, higher up the slope, hoping for a break in the clouds, where I might see the lake that lay below us.

As I climbed, I reflected on what it must have been for our ancestors, without fire, often without shelter, wandering in nature, so beautiful and bountiful, but so pitiless in her effects. I reflected that without language, or before language, the mind cannot comfort itself.

And yet it is the language of our thoughts that tortures us more than any excess or deprivation of nature.

What would it be like – nay, what would it be? There is no like, no likeness to this question. What would it be, to be a being without language – not an animal, but something nearer to myself?

2

Here I am, in my inadequate skin, goose-fleshed and shivering. A poor specimen of a creature, with no nose of a dog, and no speed of a horse, and no wings like the invisible buzzards whose cries I hear above me like lost souls, and no fins or even a mermaid's tail for this wrung-out weather. I am not as well-found as that dormouse disappearing into a crack in the rock. I am a poor specimen of a creature, except that I can think.

In London I was not so content as I am here on the lake and in the Alps, where there is solitude for the mind. London is perpetual; a constant streaming present hurrying towards a receding future. Here, where time is neither so crammed nor so scarce, I fancy, anything might happen, anything is possible.

The world is at the start of something new. We are the shaping spirits of our destiny. And though I am not an inventor of machines I am an inventor of dreams.

Yet I wish I had a cat.

I am now above the roofline of the house, the chimneys poking through the damp cloth of steaming rain like the ears of a giant animal. My skin is covered in beads of clear water as though I have been embroidered with water. There is something fine about my decorated nakedness. My nipples are like the teats of a rain-god. My pubic hair, always thick, teems like a dark shoal. The rain increases steady as a waterfall and me inside it. My eyelids are drenched. I'm wiping my eyeballs with my fists.

3

Shakespeare. He coined that word: eyeball. What play is it in? Eyeball?

Crush this herb into Lysander's eye
Whose liquor hath this virtuous property
And make his eye-balls roll with wonted sight.

Then I see it. I think I see it. What do I seem to see?

A figure, gigantic, ragged, moving swiftly on the rocks above me, climbing away from me, his back turned to me, his movements sure, and at the same time hesitant, like a young dog whose paws are too big for him. I thought to call out but I confess I was afraid.

And then the vision was gone.

Surely, I thought, if it is some traveller who has lost his way he will find our villa. But he was climbing away, as though he had found the villa already and passed on.

Troubled that I had indeed seen a figure, equally troubled that I had imagined him, I made my return to the house. I crept in softly, this time through a side door, and, shivering with cold, I made my way up the curve of the staircase.

My husband stood on the landing. I approached him, naked as Eve, and I saw the man of him stir beneath the apron of his shirt.

I was out walking, I said.

Naked? he said.

Yes, I said.

He put out his hand and touched my face.

4

What is your substance, whereof are you made,
That millions of strange shadows on you tend?

We were all around the fire that night, the room more shadows than light, for we had few candles, and none could be fetched until the weather bettered.

Is this life a disordered dream? Is the external world the shadow, while the substance is what we cannot see, or touch, or hear, yet apprehend?

Why, then, is this dream of life so nightmarish? Feverish? Sweatish?

Or is it that we are neither dead nor alive?

A being neither dead nor alive.

All my life I have feared such a state, and so it has seemed better to me to live how I can live, and not fear death.

So I left with him at seventeen and these two years have been life to me.

In the summer of 1816 the poets Shelley and Byron, Byron's physician, Polidori, Mary Shelley and her stepsister, Claire Clairmont, by then Byron's mistress, rented two properties on Lake Geneva in Switzerland. Byron enjoyed the grand Villa Diodati, while the Shelleys took a smaller, more charming house, a little lower down the slope.

Such was the notoriety of the households that an hotel on the farther shore of the lake set up a telescope for their guests to watch the antics of the supposed Satanists and Sexualists who held their women in common.

It is true that Polidori was in love with Mary Shelley but she refused to sleep with him. Byron might have slept

5

with Percy Shelley, if Shelley had been so inclined, but there is no evidence of that. Claire Clairmont would have slept with anyone – on this occasion she slept only with Byron. The households spent all their time together – and then it started to rain.

My husband adores Byron. Each day they take a boat out on the lake, to talk about poetry and liberty, whilst I avoid Claire, who can talk about nothing. I must avoid Polidori, who is a lovesick dog.

But then the rain came, and these downpouring days allow for no lake-work.

At least the weather allows no staring at us from the farther shore either. In town I heard the rumour that a guest had spied half a dozen petticoats spread out to dry on Byron's terrace. In truth, what they saw was bed linen. Byron is a poet but he likes to be clean.

And now we are confined by innumerable gaolers, each formed out of a drop of water. Polidori has brought a girl up from the village to entertain him, and we do what we can on our damp beds, but the mind must be exercised as well as the body.

That night we sat around the steaming fire talking of the supernatural.

Shelley is fascinated by moonlit nights and the sudden sight of ruins. He believes that every building carries an imprint of the past, like a memory, or memories, and that these can be released if the time is right. But what is the right time? I asked him, and he wondered if time itself depends on those who are in time. If time uses us as channels for the past – yes, that must be so, he said, as some people can speak to the dead.

Polidori does not agree. The dead are gone. If we have souls, they do not return. The cadaver on the slab has no hope of resurrection – in this world or the next.

Byron is an atheist and does not believe in life after death. *We are haunted by ourselves*, he says, and that is enough for any man.

Claire said nothing because she has nothing to say.

The servant brought us wine. It is a relief to have a liquid that is not water.

We are like the drowned, said Shelley.

We drank the wine. The shadows make a world on the walls.

This is our Ark, I said, peopled here, afloat, waiting for the waters to abate.

What do you imagine they talked about, on the Ark, said Byron, shut in with the hot stink of animal? Did they believe that the entire earth sat in a watery envelope, like the foetus in the womb?

Polidori interrupted excitedly (he is a great one for interrupting excitedly). In medical school we had a row of just such foetuses, at varying stages of gestation, all abortions; fingers and toes curled against the inevitable, eyes closed against the light never to be seen.

The light is seen – I said – the mother's skin stretched over the growing child lets in the light. They turn in joy towards the sun.

Shelley smiled at me. When I was pregnant with William, he used to get on his knees as I sat on the edge of the bed and hold my stomach in his hands like a rare book he hadn't read.

This is the world in little, he said. And that morning, oh I remember it, we sat in the sun together and I felt my baby kick for joy.

But Polidori is a doctor, not a mother. He sees things differently.

I was going to say, he said, a little resentful at being interrupted (as interrupters are wont to be), *I was going to say*, that, whether there is a soul or there is not a soul, the moment of consciousness is mysterious. Where is consciousness in the womb?

Male children are conscious earlier than female children, said Byron. I asked him what caused him to think so. He replied, The male principle is readier and more active than the female principle. This we observe in life.

We observe that men subjugate women, I said. I have a daughter of my own, said Byron. She is docile and passive.

Ada is but six months old! And you have not seen her at all since shortly after she was born! What child, male or female, does more than sleep and suck when it is born? That is not their sex; it is their biology!

Ah, said Byron, I thought she would be a glorious boy. If I must sire girls, then I trust she will marry well.

Is there not more to life than marriage? I asked.

For a woman? said Byron. Not at all. For a man, love is of his life, a thing apart. For a woman, it is her whole existence.

8

My mother, Mary Wollstonecraft, would not agree with you, I said.

And yet she tried to kill herself for love, said Byron.

Gilbert Imlay. A charmer. A chancer. A mercenary. A man of mercurial mind and predictable behaviour (why is it so often so?). My mother jumping off a bridge in London, her skirts making a parachute for her falling body. She did not die. No, she did not die.

That came later. Giving birth to me.

Shelley saw my hurt and discomfort. When I read your mother's book, said Shelley, looking at Byron, not at me, I was convinced by her.

I loved him for that – then and now – he first told me so when I was a young girl of sixteen, and the proud daughter of Mary Wollstonecraft and William Godwin.

Mary Wollstonecraft: A *Vindication of the Rights of Woman.* 1792.

Your mother's work, said Shelley, shy and confident in that way of his, your mother's work is remarkable.

Would that I might do something myself, I said, to be worthy of her memory.

Why is it that we wish to leave some mark behind? said Byron. Is it only vanity?

No, I said, it is hope. Hope that one day there will be a human society that is just.

That will never happen, said Polidori. Not unless every human being is wiped away and we begin again.

Wipe every human being away, said Byron; yes, why not? And so we are back to our floated Ark. God had the right idea. Begin again.

Yet he saved eight, said Shelley, for the world must be peopled.

We are a little half-ark here ourselves, are we not? observed Byron. We four in our watery world.

Five, said Claire.

I forgot, said Byron.

There will be a revolution in England, said Shelley, as there has been in America, and in France, and then, truly, we shall begin again.

And how shall we avoid what follows revolution? We have witnessed the French problem in our own lifetime. Firstly the Terror, where every man becomes a spy against his neighbour, and then the Tyrant. Napoleon Bonaparte – is he to be preferred to a king?

The French Revolution gave nothing to the people, said Shelley – and so they look for a strong man who claims to give them what they do not have. None can be free unless first he is fed.

Do you believe that if every person had enough money, enough work, enough leisure, enough learning, that if they were not oppressed by those above them, or fearful of those below them, humankind would be perfected? Byron asked this in his negative drawl, sure of the response, and so I set out to disaffect him.

I do! I said.

I do not! said Byron. The human race seeks its own death. We hasten towards what we fear most.

I shook my head. I was on firm ground now in this ark of ours. I said, It is men who seek death. If a single one of you carried a life in his womb for nine months, only to see that child perish as a baby, or in infancy, or through want, disease, or, thereafter, war, you would not seek death in the way that you do.

Yet death is heroic, said Byron. *And life is not.*

I have heard, interrupted Polidori, I have *heard*, that some of us do not die, but live, life after life, on the blood of others. They opened a grave in Albania recently, and the corpse, though one hundred years old, yes, one hundred years old (he paused for us to marvel), was perfectly preserved, with fresh blood visible at the mouth.

Write that story, will you? said Byron. He got up and poured wine from the jug. His limp is more pronounced in the damp. His fine face was animated. Yes, I have an idea: if we are to be kept here like Arkivists let us each record a story of the supernatural. Yours, Polidori, shall be of the Undead. Shelley! You believe in ghosts . . .

My husband nodded – I have seen such, surely, but what is more frightening? A visit from the dead, or the undead?

Mary? What say you? (Byron smiled at me.)

What say I?

But the gentlemen were pouring more wine.

What say I? (To myself I say . . .) I never knew my mother. She was dead as I was born and the loss of her was so complete I did not feel it. It was not a loss outside of me – as it is when we lose someone we know. There are two people then. One who is you and one who is not you. But in childbirth there is no me/not me. The loss was inside of me as I had been inside of her. I lost something of myself.

My father did his best to care for me as a child, motherless as I was, and he did this by lavishing on my mind what he could not give to my heart. He is not a cold man; he is a man.

My mother, for all her brilliance, was the hearth of his heart. My mother was the place where he stood with the flames warming his face. She never put aside the passion and the compassion natural to a woman – and he told me that many a time when he was weary of the world, her arms around him were better than any book yet written. And I believe this as fervently as I believe in books yet to be written, and I deny that I must choose between my mind and my heart.

My husband is of this temper. Byron is of the opinion that woman is from man born – his rib, his clay – and I find this singular in a man as intelligent as he. I said, It is strange, is it not, that you approve of the creation story we read in the Bible when you do not believe in God? He smiles and shrugs, explaining – It is a metaphor for the distinctions between men and women. He turns away, assuming I have understood and that is the end of the matter, but I continue, calling him back as he limps away like a Greek god. May we not consult Doctor Polidori here, who, as a physician, must know that since the creation story no living man has yet given birth to anything living? It is you, sir, who are made from us, sir.

The gentlemen laugh at me indulgently. They respect me, up to a point, but we have arrived at that point.

We are talking about the animating principle, says Byron, slowly and patiently as if to a child. Not the soil, not the bedding, not the container; the life-spark. The life-spark is male.

Agreed! said Polidori, and of course if two gentlemen agree that must be enough to settle the matter for any woman.

Yet I wish I had a cat.

Vermicelli, said Shelley, later, in bed with me. Men have animated a piece of vermicelli. Are you jealous?

I was stroking his long, thin arms, my legs over his long, thin legs. He was referring to Doctor Darwin, who seems to have seen some evidence of voluntary motion in a piece of vermicelli.

Now you are teasing me, I said – and you, a forked biped exhibiting certain signs of involuntary motion at the junction of trunk and bifurcation.

What is it? he said, softly, kissing my hair. I know his voice when it begins to break like this.

Your cock, I said, my hand on it as it gained life.

This is sounder than galvanism, he said. And I wish he had not, for I was distracted then, thinking of Galvani and his electrodes and leaping frogs.

Why have you stopped? asked my husband.

What was his name? Galvani's nephew? The book you have at home?

Shelley sighed. Yet he is the most patient of men: *An Account of the late improvements in Galvanism with a series of curious and interesting experiments performed before the Commissioners of the French National Institute, and Repeated Lately in the Anatomical Theatres of London. To which is added an appendix, containing the author's experiments conducted on the body of a malefactor executed at Newgate . . . 1803.*

Yes, that one, I said, resuming my vigour, tho' my ardour had flowed upwards to my brain.

With a fine movement Shelley rolled me onto my back and eased himself inside me; a pleasure I did not discourage.

We have all human life here, he said, to make as we please out of our bodies and our love. What do we want with frogs and vermicelli? With grimacing, twitching corpses and electrical currents?

Did they not say, in the book, that his eyes opened? The criminal?

My husband closed his eyes. Tensing himself, he shot into me half-worlds of his to meet half-worlds of mine, and I turned my head to look out of the window where the moon was hanging like a lamp in a brief and clear sky.

What is your substance, whereof are you made,
That millions of strange shadows on you tend?

Sonnet 54, said Shelley.

Sonnet 53, I said.

He was spent. We lay looking out of the window together at the scudding clouds that speeded the moon.

And you in every blessed shape we know.

The lover's body imprinted on the world. The world imprinted on the lover's body.

On the other side of the wall the sound of Lord Byron spearing Claire Clairmont.

Such a night of moon and stars. The rain had starved us of these sights and now they seemed more wonderful. The light fell on Shelley's face. How pale he is!

I said to him, Do you believe in ghosts? Truly?

I do, he said, for how can it be that the body is master of the spirit? Our courage, our heroism, yes, even our hatreds, all that we do that shapes the world – is that the body or the spirit? It is the spirit.

I considered this and replied, If a human being ever succeeded in reanimating a body, by galvanism or some method yet undiscovered, would the spirit return?

I do not believe so, said Shelley. The body fails and falls. But the body is not the truth of what we are. The spirit will not return to a ruined house.

How would I love you, my lovely boy, if you had no body?

Is it my body that you love?

And how can I say to him that I sit watching him while he sleeps, while his mind is quiet and his lips silent, and that I kiss him for the body I love?

I cannot divide you, I said.

He wrapped his long arms around me and rocked me in our damp bed. He said, I would, if I could, when my body fails, cast my mind into a rock or a stream or a cloud. My mind is immortal – I feel it to be.

Your poems, I said. They are immortal.

Perhaps, he said. But something more. How can I die? It is impossible. Yet I shall die.

How warm he is in my arms. How far from death.

Did you think of a story yet? he said.

I said, Nothing comes when bidden and I lack the power of imagination.

The dead or the undead? he said. A ghost or a vampyre; what will you choose?

What would frighten you most of all?

He pondered this for a moment, turning on his elbow to face me, his face so close I could breathe him in. He said, A ghost, however awful or ghastly its appearance, however dreadful its utterances, would awe me but would not terrify me, for it has been alive once, as I have, and passed into spirit, as I will, and its material substance is no more. But a vampyre is a filthy thing, a thing that feeds its decayed body on the vital bodies of others. Its flesh is colder than death, and it has no pity, only appetite.

The Undead, then, I said, and, as I lay with my eyes open wide with thinking, he fell asleep.

Our first child died when he was born. Cold and tiny I held him in my arms. Soon after I dreamed that he was not dead, and that we rubbed him with brandy and set him by the fire and he returned to life.

It was his little body I wanted to touch. I would have given him my own blood to restore his life; he had been of my blood, a feeding vampyre, for nine dark months in his hiding place. The Dead. The Undead. Oh, I am used to death and I hate it.

I got up, too restless to sleep, and, covering my husband, wrapped a shawl round me and stood at the window, looking out over the dark shadows of the hills and the glittering lake.

Perhaps it would be fine tomorrow.

My father sent me away for a time to live in Dundee with a cousin, whose company, he hoped, would improve my solitude. But there is something of a lighthousekeeper in me, and I am not afraid of solitude, nor of nature in her wildness.

I found in those days that my happiest times were outside and alone, inventing stories of every kind, and as far from my real circumstances as possible. I became my own ladder and trapdoor to other worlds. I was my own disguise. The sight of a figure, far off, on some journey of his own, was enough to spark my imagination towards a tragedy or a miracle.

I was never bored except in the company of others.

And at home, my father, who had little interest in what was fit or otherwise for a young, motherless girl, allowed me to sit unseen and silent while he entertained his friends, and they spoke of politics, of justice, and more than that too.

The poet Coleridge was a regular visitor to our house. One evening he read out loud his new poem

The Rime of the Ancient Mariner. It begins – how well I recall it –

> *It is an ancient Mariner,*
> *And he stoppeth one of three.*
> *'By thy long grey beard and glittering eye,*
> *Now wherefore stopp'st thou me?*

I crouched behind the sofa, a mere girl, enthralled to hear the tale told to the wedding guest and to picture in my mind the awful journey at sea.

The Mariner is under a curse for killing the friendly bird, the albatross, that followed the ship in better days.

In a scene most terrible, the ship, with its tattered sails and battered decks, is crewed by its own dead, reanimated in fearful force, unhallowed and dismembered, as the vessel drives forth to the land of ice and snow.

He has violated life, I thought, then and now. But what is life? The body killed? The mind destroyed? The ruin of Nature? Death is natural. Decay inevitable. There is no new life without death. There can be no death unless there is life.

The Dead. The Undead.

The moon was clouded over now. Rain clouds rapidly returned to the clear sky.

If a corpse returned to life, would it be alive?

If the doors of the charnel house opened and we dead awakened . . . then . . .

My thoughts are fevered. I hardly know my mind tonight.

*

There is something at work in my soul which I do not understand.

What do I fear most? The dead, the undead, or, a stranger thought . . . that which has never been alive?

I turned to look at him sleeping, motionless, yet living. The body in sleep is a comfort although it mimics death. If he were dead, how should I live?

Shelley, too, was a visitor to our house; that is how I met him. I was sixteen. He was twenty-one. A married man.

It was not a happy marriage. He wrote of his wife, Harriet: *I felt as if a dead and living body had been linked together in loathsome and horrible communion.*

It was on a night when he walked forty miles to his father's house – in that night and dreamlike trance he believed he had *already met the female destined to be mine.*

Soon enough we met.

When my household duties were done, I had the habit of slipping away to my mother's grave in St Pancras churchyard. There, I pursued my reading, propped against her headstone. Soon Shelley began to meet me in secret; my mother's blessing on us, I believe, as we sat either side of the grave, talking of poetry and revolution. Poets are the unacknowledged legislators of life, he said.

I used to wonder about her in her coffin below. And I never thought of her as rotted, but as alive as she is in the pencil drawings of her, and more alive yet in her writings. Even so, I wanted to be near to her body. Her poor body no use to her now. And I felt, and I am certain that Shelley felt it too, that we were there all three of us, at the grave. There was comfort in it, and not of God or heaven, but that she was alive to us.

I loved him for bringing her back to me. He was neither ghoulish nor sentimental. Last resting place. He is my resting place.

I was aware that my father had secured her body against the diggers and the robbers who take any corpse they can for ready money, and they are rational enough – what use is the body when it is no use at all?

In dissecting theatres all over London there are bodies of mothers, bodies of husbands, bodies of children, like mine, taken for liver and spleen, to crush the skull, saw the bones, unwind the secret miles of intestine.

The deadness of the dead, said Polidori, is not what we fear. Rather we fear that they are not dead when we lay them in that last chamber. That they awake to darkness, and suffocation, and so die in agony. I have seen such agony in the faces of some new-buried and brought in for dissection.

Have you no conscience? I said. No scruples?

Have you no interest in the future? he said. The light of science burns brightest in a blood-soaked wick.

*

The sky above me severed in forked light. The electrical body of a man seemed to be for a second lit up and then dark. Thunder over the lake, then, coming again, the yellow zig and zag of electrical force. From the window I saw a mighty shadow toppling down like a warrior slain. The thud of the fall shook the window. Yes. I see it. A tree hit by lightning.

Then the rain again like a million miniature drummers drumming.

My husband stirred but did not wake. In the distance the hotel flashed into view, deserted, blank-windowed and white, like the palace of the dead.

Strange shadows on you tend . . .

I must have gone back to bed, for I woke again, upright, my hair down, my hand clutching the bed curtain.

I had dreamed. Had I dreamed?

I saw the pale student of unhallowed arts kneeling beside the thing he had put together. I saw the hideous phantom of a man stretched out, and then, on the working of some powerful engine, show signs of life, and stir with an uneasy, half-vital motion.

Such success would terrify the artist; he would rush away from his odious handiwork, horror-stricken. He would hope that, left to itself, the slight spark of life which he had communicated would fade; that the thing which had received such imperfect animation would subside into dead matter, and he might sleep in the belief that the silence of the grave would quench forever the transient existence of the hideous corpse which he had

21

looked upon as the cradle of life. He sleeps, but he is awakened; he opens his eyes, behold, the horrid thing stands at his bedside, opening his curtains, and looking on him with yellow, watery, but speculative eyes.

I opened mine in terror.

On the morrow I announced that I had *thought of a story*.

Story: a series of connected events, real or imagined. Imagined or real.

Imagined
And
Real

Reality bends in the heat.

I'm looking through a shimmer of heat at buildings whose solid certainties vibrate like sound waves.

The plane is landing. There's a billboard:
Welcome to Memphis, Tennessee.
I'm here for the global Tec-X-Po on Robotics.

Name?
Ry Shelley.
Exhibitor? Demonstrator? Purchaser?
Press.
Yes, I have you here, Mr Shelley.
It's Dr Shelley. The Wellcome Trust.
You're a doctor?
I am. I'm here to consider how robots will affect our mental and physical health.
That is a good question, Dr Shelley. And let's not forget the Soul.
I'm not sure that's my area . . .
We all have a Soul. Hallelujah. Now, who are you here to interview?
Ron Lord.

(Short pause while the database finds Ron Lord.)

Yes. Here he is. Exhibitor Class A. Mr Lord will be waiting for you at the Adult Futures Suite. Here is a map. My name is Claire. I am your point of contact today.

Claire was tall, black, beautiful, well-dressed in a tailored dark green skirt and pale green silk shirt. I felt glad that she was my point of contact today.

Claire wrote out my name-badge with a brisk, manicured hand. Handwriting – a strangely old-fashioned and touching method of identification at a futuristic tech expo.

Claire – excuse me – my name – not Ryan, just Ry.

I apologise, Dr Shelley, I am not familiar with English names – and you are English?

Yes, I am.

Cute accent. (I smile. She smiles.)

Is this your first time in Memphis?

Yes, it is.

You like BB King? Johnny Cash? And THE King?

Martin Luther King?

Well, sir, I was talking about Elvis – but now you bring it to my attention, we do seem to have a lotta Kings here – maybe something about calling this city Memphis – I guess if you name a place after the capital of Egypt, you gonna see some pharaohs – uh-huh?

Naming is power, I say to her.

It sure is. Adam's task in the Garden of Eden.

Yes, indeed, to name everything after its kind. Sexbot . . .

Pardon me, sir?

26

Do you think Adam would have thought of that? Dog, cat, snake, fig tree, sexbot?

I am thankful he didn't have to, Dr Shelley.

Yes, I am sure you are right. So tell me, Claire, why did they call this place Memphis?

You mean back in 1819? When it was founded?

As she speaks I see in my mind a young woman looking out of a sodden window across the lake.

I say to Claire, Yes. 1819. *Frankenstein* was a year old.

She frowns. I am not following you, sir.

The novel *Frankenstein* – it was published in 1818.

The guy with the bolt through his neck?

More or less . . .

I saw the TV show.

It's why we are here today. (There was a look of confusion on Claire's face as I said this, so I explained.) I don't mean existentially Why We Are Here Today – I mean why the Tec-X-Po is here. In Memphis. It's the kind of thing organisers like; a tie-in between a city and an idea. Memphis and *Frankenstein* are both two hundred years old.

Your point?

Tech. AI. Artificial Intelligence. *Frankenstein* was a vision of how life might be created – the first non-human intelligence.

What about angels? (Claire looks at me, serious and certain. I hesitate . . . What is she saying?)

27

Angels?

That's right. Angels are non-human intelligence.

Oh, I see. I meant the first non-human intelligence created by a human.

I have been visited by an angel, Dr Shelley.

That's wonderful, Claire.

I don't hold with Man playing God.

I understand. I hope I haven't offended you, Claire?

She shook her head of shiny hair and pointed to the map of the city. You asked me why they called it Memphis, back in 1819 – and the answer is because we are on a river – the Mississippi – and the old Memphis was on the River Nile – you seen Elizabeth Taylor playing Cleopatra?

Yes, I have.

You know, she wore her own jewels? Think of that.

(I thought of it.)

Yes, all her own jewels, and most of them bought by Richard Burton. He was English.

Welsh.

Where is Wales?

It is in Britain but it isn't in England.

I find that confusing.

United Kingdom: the UK is made up of England, Scotland, a slice of Ireland, and Wales.

I see . . . OK. Well. I'm not visiting any time soon, so I don't have to worry about directions. Now, here, see the map, here where we are now? This is a delta region also, like the region of the Nile around the first Memphis.

Have you been to Egypt?

No, but I have been to Vegas. Very lifelike. Very Egypt.

I hear they have an animatronic Sphinx in Vegas.

Yes, they do.

You could call that a robot.

You could. I don't.

Do you know everything about this place? Your Memphis?

I like to think so, Dr Shelley. If you are interested in Martin Luther King, you should visit the National Civil Rights Museum right on the site of the Lorraine Motel, where he was shot dead. You been there yet?

Not yet.

You been to Graceland though?

Not yet.

Beale Street? Home of the Memphis Blues?

Not yet.

You got a lotta Not Yets in your life, Dr Shelley.

She's right. I am liminal, cusping, in between, emerging, undecided, transitional, experimental, a start-up (or is it an upstart?) in my own life.

I said, One life is not enough . . .

She nodded at me. Uh-huh. *Ain't that the truth?* That is the truth. But don't despair. Way over yonder is life without end.

Claire looked into the middle distance, her eyes shining with certainty. She asked me if I would like to go with her to her church on Sunday. A real church, she said, not a white man's whitewash.

A beep on her headset crackled an instruction I couldn't hear. She turned away from me to make an announcement over the tannoy.

My mind idled around the difference between desire for life without end and desire for more than one life, that is, more than one life, but lived simultaneously.

I could be me and me too. If I could make copies of myself – upload my mind and 3D-print my body, then one Ry could be in Graceland, another Ry at the shrine of Martin Luther King, a third Ry busking the Blues in Beale Street. Later, all my selves could meet, share the day, and reassemble into the original self I like to believe is me.

What is your substance, whereof are you made,
That millions of strange shadows on you tend?

Claire turned back to me, smiling. I said, mostly to myself, *I don't want to live forever.*

What's that you say? She leaned forward, frowning.

I said, Life without end. I don't want to live forever.

Claire nodded and raised her perfect eyebrow.

Uh-huh. I'm going to be with Jesus, but you can suit yourself.

Thank you, Claire. Have you taken a tour around the expo?

I am a venue expert, not a host, so I am not expected to have detailed knowledge of the events here.

Have you seen any of the robots?

Robots are serving in the cafeteria. It's not a good experience.

Why not, Claire?

They bring your eggs, and when you say, Excuse me! Hey! I didn't order tomatoes! They say, Thanks, Ma'am. Have A Nice Day! And glide away to the water fountain. They glide because they can't walk yet.

No, they can't walk yet. Walking is hard for bots. But be patient, Claire, and remember – bots find the unexpected difficult to process.

Claire looked at me like I'm in Special Needs.

You call a tomato The Unexpected?

Not the tomato – your response to the tomato.

Claire shook her head. Y'know, Doc, my mom worked in a late-nite diner all her life. 6 p.m. to 6 a.m. to feed her family. She could throw out the drunk guys with one hand and give the hungry kids an extra helping with the other hand. She wasn't an educated woman, but there was nothing artificial about her intelligence.

That's one view, I said. I respect it.

I am not even supposed to be here, said Claire. I'm emergency support. I am on release from the World Championship Barbecue Cooking Contest.

Wow! Champion Barbecue Person!

Yes, said Claire, in full flow. We get over 100,000 visitors a year here in Memphis for the championship – it's a real big barbecue scene – didn't you know?

No, I didn't know.

I started in Sauce – I managed the Sauce Wrestling –
that's forty gallons of barbecue sauce in a giant vat and in
you go. Yes! Right in! Fight it out! It's messy but it's fun.

Claire, have you personally fought in a vat of sauce?

Personally? Dr Shelley, no.

But you are the champion!

No! I organise the competition.

Oh. I see. (Pause.) Is it flavoured? The sauce?

Sure is! Takes weeks to get the taste off your skin and
every dog in town follows you home. Four legs and two,
know what I mean? I manage the entire event now –
entirely. Sponsorship, demos, games, prizes.

That's impressive, Claire.

Yes, it is. I am an expert in my own field.

You look like an expert. Maybe it's the way you style
your hair. Very professional hair.

Thank you, Dr Shelley. Anything you want to ask me?

Would you like to come around the show with me?
Might make you feel better about it. I can explain a few
things. I know a few things about – (not love) – robotics.

I am a Christian, Dr Shelley.

There is nothing in the Bible against robots.

It says in the Bible that thou shalt not make unto thee
a graven image. That is one of the Ten Commandments.

Is a robot a graven image, Claire?

It's a ballpark likeness of a God-given human.

A likeness that comes to life?

I wouldn't call it life. We're fooling ourselves if we
call a robot alive. Only God can create life.

Claire, are you sure?

I don't want to take any chances, Dr Shelley. I have to think of my eternity.

That's certainly taking the long view . . .

Yes, it is.

A young woman wearing tight leather trousers and an oversize buckskin fringed jacket rushed up to the desk, interrupting without even noticing she was interrupting.

She said, I'm looking for Intelligent Vibrators. Where are they?

Claire took a breath before she answered. Ma'am, are you an exhibitor, a demonstrator or a purchaser?

I have an emergency!

What kinda emergency?

The woman shuddered inside her leather and buckskin as she said, I have accidentally posted pictures of myself, mostly naked, except for two tassels, using the Intelligent Vibrator, on my Facebook page.

That wasn't very intelligent, I said.

The woman glared at me.

It's a privacy infringement! I need to speak to the demonstrator at the stand. They showed me how to work the camera on the vibrator. I knew it had a remote control. They didn't tell me it would remotely upload to my default app if I didn't reset it.

Claire pursed her lips and went to her screen. I could see her manicured fingertips tapping out Intelligent Vibrator. I asked the woman – because I had to know –

33

why would anyone want a vibrator featuring a camera and a remote control?

She looked at me with a mixture of anger and contempt. She said, Teledildonics.

Pardon me?

She said, Haven't you *heard* of teledildonics?

Sadly, never. But I am British.

She raised the kind of eyebrow that says: *What are you even doing here, dude?*

She sighed. (Heavily.) She said, The idea, the *idea*, is sexplay with your partner, or partners, from separate locations. It feels like they are in the room – doing things to you.

Does it?

Yes, it does. And you can share the photos.

With all your friends on Facebook?

Actually, this is none of your business, OK?

It's a bit late to be asking for privacy.

I thought she was going to hit me. Fortunately Claire swung back into the zone.

Your name, miss?

Polly D. Just the initial D. I am on the list.

We don't have a list, ma'am.

The VIP list. I work for *Vanity Fair*.

We don't have a VIP list, Miss D. I have paged the company. A representative from **IN-VIBE** is coming right now.

Haha – good pun, Claire, I said.

Now Claire was glaring at me too. She folded her arms in a goodbye-and-get-lost kind of a way.

I have to do my job, Dr Shelley, and I guess you have to do yours. The Adult Futures Suite is to your left and signposted.

Is he in pornography? said Polly D. I mean, he's obviously not a real doctor. What is he? Some kind of Dr Jackoff?

I ignored her. Thanks for your help, Claire. Good luck, Polly.

I turned away, hearing:

Asshole!

On the way to the Adult Futures Suite I pass the Singularity Suite. There's a large screen showing an interview between Elon Musk and Ray Kurzweil talking about the Singularity – the moment when AI changes the way we live, forever. Some young guys are wearing T-shirts with the slogan 'Give Up Meat'.

It's not that the future will be vegetarian – just that they believe that soon enough the human mind – our minds – will no longer be tied to a body that is a substrate made of meat.

But for now we are still human, all too human (strange phrase, that, when you think about it), and eighty per cent of internet traffic is pornography. The first non-biological life forms sharing our homes won't be waiters with tomato-recognition issues, or cute little ETs for the kids. Let's start at the very beginning: a very good place to start. Sex.

The guy waving two cell phones and wearing a headset sweeps me inside the Adult Futures Suite. He's got the body and build of a nightclub bouncer: broad chest, overweight, short legs, thick arms, sweaty in a crumpled suit. Coke cans line the coffee table in front of the couch. Ron Lord snaps open two more and hands one to me.

It's a long way from Three Cocks, eh, Ryan?

I beg your pardon?

Three Cocks. The village in Wales where I started the future.

That's a big claim, Ron.

I think big, Ryan. Google Maps. See for yourself. Three Cocks. My mum's a bit psychic. She said it was a sign. Three Cocks is where I built my first sexbot. Mail-order doll. All her parts arrived in separate bags like a chainsaw massacre. I put her together with one screwdriver and the instruction video. Really, it's Lego for adults.

I knew you'd started at the bottom, I said to Ron.

Yeah, it was her bottom where I started, said Ron.

Sitting on the couch was a human-scale doll with soft brown hair falling onto her shoulders. The doll was wearing double-denim, shorts and jacket, and underneath a pink top stretched across breasts the size of lifebuoys.

Is that her? Your first one?

Show some respect, Ryan! My first is retired. She wasn't even a commercial variety. I still have her and I love her, but she's archive now. This one here, she's part of my franchise range.

Watch this! Ready? Film it on your phone! Go on!

Ron swings up the doll from the couch and points to a bright pink mat underneath her. The mat says PUSSY.

You see this mat? says Ron. This is a SmartMat. This mat powers her up while she sits next to you. You can have it in the car too – works on the cigarette-lighter socket. Electrodes in her bum.

Look at this – (swipes iPad with fat finger) – here's the factory in China where the dolls are made. Torso comes through first, swinging on the overhead wires, complete with two holes, user-ready, and F-cup moulded tits. I am working on a model with detachable tits, for variety, but they don't make that in China yet, too specialist. Anyway, torso, torso, another torso (he swipes impatiently). Here we are! See how they attach the arms? Lovely slim arms. Then the legs. Look at the length! The shape! Slightly longer than they would be if she was human. This is fantasy, not nature, so you can have what you want. Hair goes on last, after the eyelashes. See the eyes? Like Bambi for boys.

Ron put the doll back down on the couch, and swigged his Coke. He said, Lightweight too. Makes a man feel strong.

So how does a sex-doll franchise work? I said.

*

The way I see it, said Ron, there's two ways to go with sexbots: buy her and own her – like I did – bring her in for a service once or twice a year, depending on wear and tear. Online you can order spare parts, if any of her gets damaged, or too messy. That's one way to enjoy an XX-BOT. We also offer trade-ins and upgrades. Very flexible.

The other way to enjoy an XX-BOT, more modern, to my mind, is rental. And if you rent, you need somewhere to rent her from, right? That's how I came up with the idea of the franchise that I'm selling here.

Your XX-BOTs?

Right, Ryan! Good name?

Good name, Ron.

You see, Ryan, renting gives you all the pleasure and none of the problems. Breakages, storage, updating – the technology is changing all the time.

And most people only buy one bot, for personal use, but what if you're having a party? With your mates? They'll all want a try.

Renting is popular with stag weekends; get half a dozen of the girls in for fun and frolics. Different models too, blonde and busty, brunette and sporty. Whatever. And what if you're the kind of bloke that only wants a bot when the wife is away? Women aren't at home all the time like they used to be. I don't blame them; women aren't goldfish. They've evolved. But, like my mum says, emancipation can be a problem for a man.

Renting a bot when you're on your lonesome is safer and cheaper than the human alternative. No diseases, no revenge porn, no getting robbed of your Rolex at 2 a.m. One business lady I know personally, a high-powered lady, she books ahead quarterly.

What? Yes! That's what I'm saying, Ryan. She books an XX-BOT for her man. He loves it. He never knows which model he's going to get. It's a bond between them. Quite touching, I think, something they do together.

With a rental, every girl gets hygiene-checked, bathed, perfumed, yeah, you can choose one of four scents – musky, floral, woody or lavender. When you pick her up she'll be wearing either double-denim like this one – or a simple day dress. You can hire or buy other outfits.

What? Yeah, just like Barbie. Yeah, I suppose you're right, it's a joke, isn't it, how boys don't get to play with Barbie till they're grown up? Haha, I hadn't thought of that – it's a thought. I hadn't thought of it but it's a thought. My mum will laugh when I tell her. Oh, yeah, my mum is a big part of the business. From day one.

Anyway, the girls we rent out get time off for education too – we're always improving their circuit boards. They don't have a big vocabulary, no; you watch porn, don't you, so you know it's not exactly a language-lab? But we're on it – men do like to communicate. It's not just 'Hello, Big Boy'.

What did you say? At the airport? Funny you should say that because that's what's next. I'm looking to go in with some of the car-hire companies – yeah, like Avis – and your car can have your XX-BOT ready and waiting, fully charged, in the passenger seat.

XX-BOTs make a great travel choice. No nagging about stopping for lunch or needing the toilet. No sulking about the Holiday Inn you've booked. She's next to you, long hair, long legs, you choose the music, beautiful woman in the passenger seat.

If you want to be a bit more discreet you can fold her up and strap her in the back, or stow her out of sight in the boot or trunk or whatever you call it. We're not all extroverts.

Here, look, watch this! See it? Yeah! I'll do it again. Are you filming this? Watch the movement. So smooth. Legs up and over. Now she's in half. You'd need to date a bloody stuntwoman to manage that.

Amazing! Eh, Ryan? Like a Brompton bicycle!

When driverless cars really take off, the client could get in the back with his XX-BOT and have a much pleasanter journey. Takes all the stress out of travel.

I'm talking to Uber.

Yeah. I have based my franchise model on the rent-a-car business. Pick up in one city, drop off in another. And I've got five styles of XX-BOTs – including the Economy model here on the couch. She's the cheapest.

She's got nylon hair, so you can get a bit of static, and she whirrs a bit, but she's a good, straightforward, no-frills, budget fuck.

See? Three holes all the same size. No! Not in the same place! You have slept with a woman, haven't you, Ryan? Well, where do you think the holes are?

Front. Back. Mouth. Not her nostrils! She's not a fuckin' yeti!

OK! You were making a joke. I get it. Now concentrate – put your finger in there!

Like it? And they all VI-BRATE! Any hole, any position. Vibrate!

Nice limb movement too. You can position her how you want. All the girls have an extra-wide splayed-leg position. It's popular with our clients, especially the fat ones.

This one can talk too. Limited but adequate voice response – like meeting a girl abroad who doesn't speak much English.

Does she have a name, Ron?

Ron nodded approvingly. That's a good question, Ryan. And I've got a good answer. I made the decision not to give my girls names. No, it's not like lambs you'll be eating later, actually it's like those very fancy paints you can buy – top-end paint – yes, we've just redecorated at home – I mean the paints that use numbers, because what a colour means to me won't be what a colour means to you – and you might be colour-blind anyway. I mean, what the fuck is Moody Blue? Wimborne White? Does Wimborne White sound gay to you? It does to me. And Donkey Brown? Since when was all donkeys the same brown? My dad kept donkeys – yeah – it's a long story. No need to go into that today. It's not about me.

*

So with the girls, I can call them Volcano, or Autumn or Cheri or whatever, but the customer might want to call his night-bird Julie . . . So we leave it to the customer to name his bird.

You're not meant to call women 'birds' nowadays, are you? I always liked it. Sums women up – not in a bad way, don't get me wrong. Birds . . . always out of reach. Aren't they? You think she's on your arm and then she's flown.

And they seem to like worms.

So, Ryan, back to my Economy model. In motor-vehicle parlance, she's the cloth-seats and plastic-steering-wheel version. But she gets you from A to B.

This model only comes in white.

My sister-in-law's a lovely black woman from Jamaica and she said to me, she said, Ron! Don't you dare do an Economy black woman. And I love women, I do, and I thought, yeah, show respect. Also, Bridget would knock the shit out of me.

Shall we have a look at Cruiser? Over by the window. Right little motor boat, this one. Like the girl next door but dirty. Cruiser's got the fuller figure. Nicely pneumatic. She's padded to give a softer feel. Those breasts are like pillows. It was Mum's idea. She said to me, Ron, some men want to curl up and fall asleep, like they did when they were little boys.

Feel these! Top-grade silicon nipples. No plastic – like fuckin' thimbles, plastic nipples. Gotta have some give. That's the key if you like breasts, and I'm a breast man myself.

Walk round the back. Go on! I'll lift the dress. Yes! Thongs. Very popular. Lovely ass with a bit of movement – soft silicon. Bigger battery so we can warm up certain parts of her skin.

My girls can seem lower-temperature than born and bred girls. All right, they *are* colder than born and bred. Flesh is flesh. But my girls are not clammy underneath you, like the bloody blow-up things – it was like lying on seaweed. God, I hated blow-up dolls, did you? Might as well wrap your dick in cling film.

So, Ryan, moving swiftly on. This one here in the tennis outfit bending over to pick up a couple of balls. She's our Racy model.

Very tight figure – little waist, double-G-cup – and I tell you what, her tits and her pussy are always warm. It's the battery plus the thermal layer. Battery life is up to three hours. I mean, men come in about four minutes, so this is generous. You can have a party, pass her around, play a hand of cards in between without worrying about her going flat. In the beginning when they went flat they slurred their words, and you could hear them whirring as well. It didn't put anyone off, but it didn't feel professional to me.

Do you like her slingback tennis shoes? Economy doesn't wear shoes. It's cute, like that French musical, *Les Misérables*.

Speaking French, I don't know if you've ever had sex with a bot – be my guest later – but I tell you there's none of that *Bonjour Tristesse* afterwards, and none of that doubt about whether she's had an orgasm or not. All my girls orgasm when you do.

Yeah, well spotted, Ryan. She certainly is. Racy is taller than the others. She's about 5 foot 4 inches – the others are about 5 foot 2 inches. We make them smaller for the Chinese and Asian markets. These are the US and UK models.

I have thought about doing a supermodel size, but it's not practical. The only point of a supermodel in real life is to show her off to your mates – I mean, she's too anorexic for anything else. Won't eat, won't drink, won't, well, you know – they are so picky. My girls are practical – they are built to work – so we keep 'em handy-sized.

Yeah, it's true, there are some really small girls on the market – they look like children. I don't get involved. I got standards.

You *can* buy some bots with Family Mode; they can talk about animals, and tell fairy stories, all that stuff, like Emmanuelle Does Disney. I'm strictly Adult. No blurred lines. So, as yet, we've got no plans for a travel doll.

Are you still recording? Good.

Just behind the screen here is a bed – for display purposes only, so don't take your shoes off, Ryan. Imagine coming home to this beauty. In fact, I do come home to this beauty. I have a Deluxe for personal use.

She's got everything you get with Racy, minus the muscles – I mean, they're all firm, but smooth and curvy, no weightlifters. Anyway, Deluxe, like the name suggests, has better quality materials all round. And Real Hair.

Where? On her head, where d'you think? You have slept with women, haven't you?

Jesus, no, I wouldn't put real hair down *there*! Or any hair, as it happens. You'd have it sopping wet and rotten in no time.

We ask for double the deposit on this model because of the hair and you have to sign a waiver declaring that you won't spill booze or smear food, piss, shit or cum in her hair.

Do they do that kind of thing? Sad but true. I wouldn't, but some do.

With nylon hair it doesn't matter much what you do – and it's cheap to replace. We rip it right off and we start again. But the good stuff, the real stuff – I mean, I am on the side of the women, I am. Who wants some twat to cum in their real hair?

Yeah . . . Horrible.

Personally, as a woman, even though I'm not, I'd hate it if some random bloke wanted to cum anywhere except the usual place, but I'm a fussy eater. Don't like yoghurt or custard, or that French one, crème brûlée, or tapioca or white sauce or suet. I don't really like banana smoothies and I hate almond milk. God, almond milk. Why??? For fuck's sake! My doctor tried to get me on it. Cholesterol. I said, mate, I'd rather have the heart attack.

Deluxe has a big vocabulary. About 200 words. Deluxe will listen to what you want to talk about – football, politics or whatever. She waits till you're finished, of course, no interrupting, even if you waffle a bit, and then she'll say something interesting.

What like? Oh, well, something like: *Ryan, you're so clever. Ryan, I hadn't thought about it like that. Do you know anything about Real Madrid?*

Yeah – that's what I mean about education. Climate change. Brexit. Football. This model is a companion – and that's how we'll forward her career as the technology develops.

Some men want more than sex. I get that.

And over to Vintage. I love the two-piece suit and pillbox hat. I got this idea from the retro-porn sites. She's late to the game but she brings plenty to the party.

We had a lot of older men asking us for something sexy and young – most old blokes aren't rich enough to get a real-life version – you need a lotta money for young girl/old man in real life. And let's face it; men prefer a box of strawberries to a plate of prunes and custard.

What we offer is fantasy life, not real life.

Vintage can be ready for you like she's straight out of the 1950s. Like BBC Calling the World – you wouldn't believe how well the voice works – we got a newsreader from BBC Radio 4 to do it. Anonymous. Paid her a fortune.

Or you can have Vintage in a 60s miniskirt and love-beads, singing *I Got You Babe.* Her mouth doesn't move, but if you're fuckin' her face off you wouldn't want it to, would you?

There's even a 70s feminist version with no bra, messy hair and a dildo for anal play. Yeah! Clever! She gets to fuck you! No, I haven't tried it. I do try them all but I didn't fancy that one. In the office we called her the Germaine. She's the only one with a name. Have you read that book? My mum told me about it. I started it but it wasn't what I thought.

Who rents her? Some masochists. And a few university professors.

All of these girls come in different skin tones: black, brown or white. Plus, you can have a muff on the Vintage model if that's what you want. The old porn stars had beavers like candyfloss, and some men liked it. So we can supply with or without, but only for the Vintage model. If you're not sure if you want fluff in your face, we can include a muff in the package with the correct glue. We do ask customers not to use their own glue. Glue on the wrong side means you get a stick-on beard.

Do I get mostly old men? Not at all. All ages and stages, Ryan; sex is a democracy. With the old blokes, I see it as a public service. You should write about that. We always offer ten per cent off to the over-sixty-fives, and there's an extra ten per cent off on Mondays. Not many people want a shag on a Monday.

Tell you what, though – and this is a bit philosophical, but I am a thinking man – there's no such thing as underage sex when it's a bot. I mean, there's no can't do it till you're sixteen or whatever, so we get some schoolkids wanting a try – yeah, boys, 'course it's boys – and I reckon it's better than sticking it up some girl who's dry as sandpaper and doesn't fancy you.

Yeah, you can be old, you can be ugly, you can be fat, smelly, you can have an STD, you can be broke. Whether you can't get it up, or you can't get it down, there's an XX-BOT for you.

Public service. I tell you, it is. Do you think I might get an MBE? Mum would love that.

Women? What about women? Are you a feminist, Ryan? I'm not, but my mum is, so don't think we haven't heard about this back in Wales.

There *are* male bots but I don't bother with them. Why not?

Anatomy, Ryan. Basic anatomy. You must have done that when you were training to be a doctor.

Basically a boy-bot is a vibrator with a body attached. He's like a shop-window mannequin with a dick that doesn't work. No thrust. He can't shunt her from behind. She has to sit on him and bounce up and down, very tiring, or joggle him on top of her like she's blending a milkshake. Also tiring. No fun when you've had the bath, the candles, all your favourite love songs on PLAY AGAIN. The things women like to get them in the mood.

Women prefer a hand-held vibrator. Better control, better delivery, and they can watch TV at the same time. I've done the market research. Well, not me personally, my mum does that side of the business. My mum? Oh, very much so. Like I said. Day one.

And with the boy-bots it's a question of scale as much as anything. Female bots are petite – even the Swedes like 'em petite – but if you build a boy-bot small it's a turn-off, like fucking your son, and women don't get off on that, not many of 'em anyway. Women want a hunk, but if you make your bot hunky, women can't lug him around. And in a small apartment, when he's not in use, so to speak, he's in the way – y'know? I mean, he can't go out for a beer when you want some personal space.

Plus women tend to drive smaller cars, and she doesn't want to draw attention to herself trying to squash some Dwayne 'The Rock' Johnson into her Renault Twingo.

If we get into nightclubs – and we might, because I don't know what to do with the money I'm making – then I might try hen-night specials where we supply some boy-bots to see how it goes – just for a laugh – like ride-my-pony sorta thing? Women might enjoy sitting on top if I can get the action right. I've got some ideas from when I used to repair pop-up toasters.

This market is global. This market is the future.

Let me tell you something about China, Ryan. That one-child policy? Thank God they've stopped it. All those strangled girl babies chucked in a paddy field somewhere. There's millions and millions of Chinese men who'll never have a female partner because there aren't enough girls to go round. That's right – what goes around comes around – like a sushi belt – you'd think they'd know that, wouldn't you? The Chinese market will be mega. That's why they've got the factories – and they love technology, and a lot of Chinese men will prefer a bot because they like the submissive type. Modern Chinese women are too independent. I went to the factory – I've seen it all.

Anyway, I'm opening my own factory in Wales. China can't have it all their own way. Show some competition, I say, and if they're in a trade war with bloody America who knows what will happen? Price of bots could go sky-high.

Mum said we should do a Karl Marx and control the means of production.

Also, I want to put something back into the community. There's no jobs in Wales, Ryan, not since Brexit. They voted Wales for the Welsh, like everyone in the world was just killing themselves to get over the border and open a new coalmine.

All the money in Wales came from some euro-fund anyway, but there's a lot of inbreeding in Wales. I think it would be good to have a bit of immigration – all that inbreeding affects the brain. Brexit! Jesus! Might as well have built a wall made out of leeks right round the place.

So I have to do my bit. I'm opening a big factory that will make the whole bot. Top to bottom. And I'm having a smaller workshop – got enterprise money for it – that just makes heads. Bit more artisan. They are quite good at handicrafts in Wales. Tea towels . . . pottery . . .

And there are a lot of out-of-work hairdressers as nobody can afford to get their hair done, not now it's just Wales for the Welsh.

50

Why do I need extra heads?

A lot of the XX-BOTs get their faces bashed in. Get thrown at the wall or something. I seriously thought about a detachable nose at one time. You can change the face yourself on some of them, but it's fiddly, and I think buying a spare head to start with is a better idea. Sex can get a bit rough, can't it? I don't judge.

Also, I'm thinking of manufacturing an Outdoor type. Tougher. Rugged. Sorta Lara Croft. We'll need our own production line for that. It might be for the fetish market. Dominatrix. Spanking. That sorta thing. The Chinese won't touch it. Brits will like it, I think. I'm in talks with Caterpillar and JCB.

This is the future, Ryan.

Are you coming to my live show? See the girls in action? Look, here's a taster on the iPad. What do you think of the music?

Walking in Memphis. I love that song. My favourite line – *There's a pretty little thing waiting for the King . . .*

They're all pretty. We're all kings.

What did you say? Does it make real life more difficult?

What is real life these days?

There never was a wilder story imagined, yet, like most of the fictions of this age, it has an air of reality attached to it.

The Edinburgh Magazine, 1818

Humankind cannot bear very much reality.

That is why we invent stories, I said.

And what if we are the story we invent? said Shelley.

Still shut in by rain, I write and write.

Claire sits sewing in a corner. Polidori nurses his lame ankle. Yesterday he jumped out of a window to prove his love for me. The idea was Byron's. When he is bored he is dangerous.

All we do is drink and fuck, said Byron. Is that a story?

That's a bestseller! said Polidori.

We sleep. We eat. We work, said Shelley.

Do you? said Byron, who is on a diet for his corpulence, and besides, he is insomniac, and idle. He cannot find the lines, he says, for his supernatural story, even though our enterprise is the challenge he set. That is irksome. We are irksome.

Polidori is busy with his own tale. He calls it *The Vampyre*. Blood transfusions interest him.

*

For want of excursion or diversion, the gentlemen fell to discussing the series of lectures we had recently attended in London. Lectures delivered by Shelley's doctor, William Lawrence, on the origin of life. Life, Doctor Lawrence argued, is based in Nature. There is no 'super-added' force such as the soul. Human beings are bone, muscle, tissue, blood, etc., and nothing more.

There was an outcry, of course: *No difference between a man and an oyster? Man is nothing more than an orang-utan or an ape, with 'ample cerebral hemispheres'?*

The Times newspaper had this to say: *Doctor Lawrence strives with all his powers to prove that men have no souls!*

Yet, I said to Shelley, you of all men believe in the soul.

I do, he said; I believe it is each man's task to awaken his own soul. His soul is that part of him not subject to death and decay; that part of him made alive to truth and beauty. If he has no soul he is a brute.

And where does this soul go, at death? said Byron.

That is unknown, answered Shelley; the *becoming* of the soul, not its going, should be our concern. The mystery of life is on earth, not elsewhere.

The rain is on earth also, said Byron, staring out of the window like a helpless god. He wanted to ride his mare and was turning restive.

We shall all be dead soon enough, said Polidori, thus we cannot live as others would wish us to live, but only for our own desires. He looked at me, his hand on his crotch.

Is there not more to life than what we desire? I said. Might we not sacrifice our own desires for some worthier cause?

You may do so if you wish, said Polidori, if that gives you satisfaction. I would rather be a vampyre than a corpse.

To die well is to live well, said Byron.

None finds satisfaction in death, replied Polidori. You imagine it so, but what will you know of it? What will you gain from it?

Reputation, said Byron.

Reputation is gossip, said Polidori. Say well of me, say ill of me – what is that but tittle-tattle?

You are out of sorts today, said Byron.

It is you who is out of sorts, said Polidori.

Shelley put his arms round me and held me to him. I love you. You, dear Mary, you, who is most alive.

I could hear Claire's needle stabbing into her tapestry.

All alive o! All alive alive o! sang Polidori, beating time on the arm of the divan. Byron scowled and limped to the window, opening it to let in the rain directly onto Claire.

Will you stop it? She jumped up as though she had been stung, shouting at his laughing at her, taking her place on another chair and savagely snipping her yarn.

Death is a counterfeit, said Shelley. Almost, I do not believe in it at all.

You will gladly believe in it when you inherit your father's estate, said Byron.

I watched him, sardonic, cynical. A great poet, truly, yet unkind. The gifts of our nature seem not to modify the manner of our behaviour.

Shelley has little money and is the most generous of men. Byron is rich, netting £10,000 a year from his estates, yet spends only for his own pleasure. He may live as he pleases. We must take care. That is, I must take care of our accounts. Shelley scarcely seems to know what he can spend and what he cannot. We are forever in debt. Still, if I can sell the story I am writing we shall be more at ease. My mother made a living from her writing. It is my intention to follow her example.

I should like to say more about the soul, said Shelley.

Byron groaned. Polidori coughed. Claire stitched viciously at her cushion cover.

My own mind, though, was elsewhere. Since I had thought of my story I had been preoccupied by it. The looming figure in my mind blotted out other concerns. My mind was in a kind of eclipse. I must return to the monstrous shadow crossing me.

I left them to their bickering and metaphysics and went upstairs to my desk with a jug of wine. Red wine eases the ache of the damp.

For the sake of my story I have my own desire to contemplate what it is about Man that distinguishes us from the rest of biology. And what distinguishes us from machines?

I visited a manufactory in Manchester with my father. I saw that the wretched creatures enslaved to the machines were as repetitive in their movements as machines. They were distinguished only by their unhappiness. The great wealth of the manufactories is not for the workers but for the owners. Humans must live in misery to be the mind of the machines.

My father had me read Hobbes' *Leviathan* when I was younger. Now I sit here, pen in hand, and into my mind comes Hobbes and his conjecture. He writes:

> *For seeing life is but a motion of Limbs, the beginning whereof is in some principall part within; why may we not say, that all Automata (Engines that move themselves by springs and wheeles as doth a watch) have an artificiall life?*

I ask myself: what is artificial life? Automata have no intelligence; they are but clockwork. Biological life, even the most wretched being, has intelligence enough to milk a cow, speak a name, know when rain will come and when it will not, reflect, perhaps, on its existence. Yet, if automata had intelligence . . . would that be sufficient to call it alive?

Shelley is improving my Greek and Latin. We lie on the bed, him naked, his hand on my back, the book on the pillow. He kisses my neck as we manage new vocabulary. Often we break off for love. I love his body. Hate it that he is so careless of himself. Truly he imagines that nothing so gross as matter can oppose him. But he is made of blood and warmth. I rest on his narrow chest, listening to his heart.

Together we are reading Ovid: *Metamorphoses.*

Italy is full of statues of beautiful men. Men who ripple and stand. To kiss one? To bring it to life?

I have touched such statues, their cold marble, their serious stone. And wrapped my arms around one and wondered at the form without the life.

Shelley read out to me from Ovid the story of the sculptor Pygmalion, who fell in love with the statue he had carved himself. So deep in love was he with his creation that women were nothing to him. He prayed to the goddess Athena that he might find a living lover as beautiful as the lifeless form on his bench. That night, he kissed the lips of the youth he had created. Hardly believing what he felt, he felt the youth kiss him in return. The cold stone warmed.

And there was more . . . Through the good offices of the goddess, the youth took on female form – a double transformation from lifeless to life and from male to female. Pygmalion married her.

It must be, said Shelley, that Shakespeare had such a picture in his mind at the close of *The Winter's Tale*, when the statue of Hermione comes to life. She steps down. She embraces her husband, Leontes, the tyrant. Through his crimes, Time itself had turned to stone, and now, in her movement, Time itself flows again. That which is lost is found.

Yes, I said. The second of warmth. To kiss the lips and find them warm.

The lips are warm after death, said Shelley. Who does not lie beside the beloved all night as the body cools? Who does not hold the body in her arms, frantic to bestow heat and reanimate the corpse? Who does not tell himself that this is but winter? In the morning surely the sun will come?

Move him into the sun, I said (I don't know why).

Artificial life. The statue wakes and walks. But what of the rest? Is there such a thing as artificial intelligence? Clockwork has no thoughts. What is the spark of mind? Could it be made? Made by us?

What is your substance, whereof are you made,
That millions of strange shadows on you tend?

The shadows darkened the corners of the room. I brooded upon the nature of my own mind. Yet when my heart stops so must my mind. No mind, however fine, outlasts the body.

My mind turned back to the journey I had made with Shelley and Claire, who returns to this story like a bookmark – not the text, but a marker of some kind.

I was to elope with Shelley, and Claire decided she could not be left behind, and so we agreed to go all together, keeping the plan secret from my father and stepmother.

I must add this note that after my mother died my father could not be alone, and soon enough he had married again – an ordinary woman of no imagination, but she could cook. She brought with her a daughter called Jane, who soon became the ardent pupil of my dead mother's writings, and in time changed her name to Claire; I did not disapprove of this. Why should she not remake herself? What is identity but what we name it? Jane/Claire acted as go-between for Shelley and myself when my father grew suspicious. Shelley and I were both fond of her, and so when the time came to leave Skinner Street it was decided that we should go together.

Stars in the sky like uncounted chances.

Four o'clock in the morning. Felt slippers on our feet, our boots in our hands, so as not to wake Father, though he sleeps deeply when he takes laudanum for his ague.

We ran through the streets where the world was waking.

We reached the coach. There was Shelley, pale and pacing, an angel without wings.

He embraced me, burying his face in my hair, whispering my name. Our modest bags were loaded, but suddenly I turned from him and ran back home, stricken with conscience, to leave my father a note on the mantelpiece. I could not break his heart. I deceive myself. I could not break his heart without telling him I was breaking his heart. We live by language.

The cat curled round my legs.

And then I was off again, running, running, my hat slipping round my neck and my breath dry in my mouth.

Anxious and exhausted, we were gone, post-haste to Dover, seasick under the sails of a boat that took us to Calais

– and my first night in his arms in a padded room in a dark inn with the rattle of iron cartwheels going over the cobbles and my heart sounding louder than iron and wheels.

This is a love story.

I could add that my stepmother soon followed us, pleading for Jane/Claire to return. I think she was glad enough to be rid of me. Shelley walked all three of us up and down separately and together, arguing love and liberty. I do not imagine she believed him, but eventually she was exhausted, and bade us farewell. He had prevailed. We were in France, the home of revolution. What could we not manage?

As it turned out – we could manage very little.

Our travels were not easy. We had no clothes. Paris was dirty and expensive. The food gave us cramps and foul smells. Shelley lived off bread and wine. I added cheese. At last we found a money-lender from whom Shelley was able to borrow sixty pounds.

Buoyed up by our wealth, we decided to travel, and set off into the country, seeking simplicity and the natural man that Rousseau had written about.

There will be beef and milk and good bread, said Shelley, and young wine and clean water.

That was the story.

The reality was otherwise.

For some weeks we endured, endeavouring to hide from each other our disappointment. This was the land of liberty. This was where my mother had come to find freedom. Where she had written *The Rights of Woman*. We thought to find like minds and open hearts. In reality, the cottagers overcharged us for every little thing. The farms were dirty and broken. The laundresses stole buttons and braids. Our guides were surly, and the donkey Shelley hired – that we might take it in turns to ride – that donkey was lame.

Does something ail you? asked Shelley, disturbed by my silences, and I did not say, yes, the sour milk the sweating cheese the rank sheets the fleas the rainstorms the rot the beds stuffed with straw stuffed with mites. The soft vegetables the gristly meat the lice-teemed fish the weevil loaves. The distress of my father. Thoughts of my mother. The state of my underclothes.

Only the heat, my love, I replied.

He asked me to bathe naked with him in the river. I was too shy. Instead I watched his body, white and slender and sculpted. There is something unworldly about his form. An approximation – as though his body has been put on hastily, so that his spirit might walk in the world.

We read Wordsworth out loud to distract the hours, but France was not poetry; it was peasants.

*

At last, knowing my distress, Shelley secured us places on a barge that floated out of France and down the Rhine.

Was it better? Smug Switzerland. Drunken Germany. More wine, I said. And so we passed our days, underfed, over-drunk, longing for the soul and not knowing where to find it.

What I want does exist if I dare to find it.

One day, not far from Mannheim, we saw the towers of a castle rising out of the mist like a warning. Shelley adores towers, woods, ruins, graveyards, any part of Man or Nature that broods.

And so we followed the track, tortuous, towards it, ignoring the staring looks of peasants at their forks and hoes.

At the foot of the castle at last we stopped and shivered. Even in the hot afternoon sun it felt cold.

What is this place? asked Shelley of a man on a cart.

Castle Frankenstein, he said.

Desolate place of brooding.

There is a story, said the man, requiring money to tell it, and Shelley paid twice over, not disappointed by what he heard.

The castle had belonged to an alchemist named Conrad Dippel. Too early his beloved wife died and, unable to bear his loss, he refused to bury her, determined to discover the secret of life.

One by one, his servants abandoned him. He lived alone, and was seen at dawn and dusk wandering amidst the graveyards and charnel houses, dragging home what fetid bodies he could find, grinding the bones of corpses to mix with fresh blood. He believed he could administer this tincture to the newly deceased and revive them.

The villagers grew to fear and hate him. Alike they must guard their dead, and alike listen for his footsteps, or the bridle bells of his horse. Many a time he burst into a house of grief. In a bottle he carried his filthy mixture, stuffing it into the slack mouth of the empty body as a goose is stuffed for liver pâté.

There was no resurrection.

At length, everyone in the surrounding villages came together and burned him alive in his castle.

The very walls reek of dismemberment and death.

I looked at the ruined place. An outside staircase, dark and tumbling, like a Piranesi nightmare, collapsed and grown through with weeds, leading spiral by spiral, step by step, down to where? What cellar of horror?

I pulled my shawl close. The air itself has the cold of the grave.

Come! I said to Shelley. We must leave this place.

He put his arm around me and together we walked swiftly away. As we walked, he instructed me in the art of alchemy.

The alchemists sought three things, said Shelley: the secret of turning lead into gold, the secret of the Elixir of Eternal Life, the homunculus.

What is an homunculus? I asked.

A creature not born of woman, he answered. A made thing, unholy and malign. A kind of goblin, misshapen and sly, infused with dark power.

In the oppressive twilight of our winding walk back to the inn I thought of that thing; that fully-formed being not born of woman.

And now that form has returned.

And it is not small. No goblin.

I feel as though my mind is a screen and on the other side of the screen there is a being seeking life. I have seen fish in an aquarium pushing their faces against the glass. I sense what I cannot say, except in the form of a story.

I will call my hero (is he a hero?) Victor – for he seeks victory over life and over death. He will strive to penetrate the recesses of Nature. He will not be an alchemist – I want no hocus-pocus here – he will be a doctor, like Polidori, like Doctor Lawrence. He will discern the course of the blood, know the knot of muscle, the density of bone, the delicacy of tissue, how the heart pumps. Airways, liquids, mass, jelly, the cauliflower mystery of the brain.

He will compose a man, larger than life, and make him live. I will use electricity. Storm, Spark, Lightning. I will rod him with fire like Prometheus. He will steal life from the gods.

At what cost?

His creature will have the strength of ten men. The speed of a galloping horse. The creature will be more than human. But he will not be human.

Yet he suffers. Suffering, I do believe, is something of the mark of the soul.

Machines do not suffer.

My creator will not be a madman. He will be a visionary. A man with family and friends. Dedicated to his work. I will take him to the brink and make him leap. I will show his glory as well as his horror.

I will call him Victor Frankenstein.

This mind is the matrix of all matter.

Max Planck

Reality cannot bear very much of humankind.

Your name?

    Ry Shelley.

Press?

    Guest. I am a guest of Professor Stein.

Professor Stein's lecture is open to the public and live-streamed on the Royal Society website.

The Royal Society was founded in 1660, for the furthering of natural science and the promotion of scientific knowledge. Here, in Carlton House Terrace, overlooking The Mall, it feels like London at its most opulent and undisturbed. In fact, the neoclassical buildings were designed by John Nash and built between 1827 and 1834. Stucco-clad. Corinthian-column facade. Elaborate frieze and pediment.

The timeless serenity of the past that we British do so well is an implanted memory – you could call it a fake memory. What seems so solid and certain is really part of the ceaseless pull-it-down-build-it-again pattern of history, where the turbulence of the past is recast as landmark, as icon, as tradition, as what we defend, what

71

we uphold – until it's time to call in the wrecking ball. In any case, the Royal Society only moved here in 1967. History is what you make it.

Tonight we are the history we are making.

I watched the audience come in: students with man-bags slung across their bodies. Hipsters with close beards. Kids in T-shirts who work at London's tech hub in Shoreditch. Sleek bankers, suave in handmade suits. Geeks. Sci-fi buffs. Two Muslim women in headscarves wearing Sophia the Robot hoodies.

There are a lot of young people in this audience.

Victor Stein has a big following on Facebook and Twitter. His TED talk has netted six million views. He's on a mission, that's certain.

Some people wonder: whose side are you on?

He'd say there are no sides – that binaries belong to our carbon-based past. The future is not biology – it's AI.

He has a nice, clear graphic up on his screen:

Type 1 Life: Evolution-based.
Victor explains: Changes happen slowly over millennia.
Type 2 Life: Partially self-designing.
This is where we are now. We can develop our own brain software through learning, including outsourcing to machines. We update ourselves individually and generationally. We can adapt within a generation to a changing world – think of toddlers and iPads. We have invented machines of every kind for travel and labour. Horses and hoes are a thing of the past. We can also

overcome some of our biological limitations: spectacles, eye-laser, dental implants, hip replacements, organ transplants, prosthetics. We have begun to explore space.

Type 3 Life: Fully self-designing.

Now he gets excited. The nearby world of AI will be a world where the physical limits of our bodies will be irrelevant. Robots will manage much of what humans manage today. Intelligence – perhaps even consciousness – will no longer be dependent on a body. We will learn to share the planet with non-biological life forms created by us. We will colonise space.

I'm watching him as he talks. I love watching him. He has that sex-mix of soul-saving and erudition. His body is lean and keen. His hair is abundant enough for vitality, grey enough for gravitas. Straight jaw, blue eyes, crisp shirt, tailored trousers tapered at the bottom, handmade shoes. Women adore him. Men admire him. He knows how to play a room. He'll walk away from the podium to make a point. He likes to crumple his notes and throw them to the floor.

He's a Gospel Channel scientist. But who will be saved?

Behind him on the screen tonight is Leonardo's drawing of *The Vitruvian Man*. As the audience sit in silence, Leonardo's image animates itself, takes an appearing trilby from an appearing peg and, placing it on the back of its head, turns and walks into an appearing sea. The sound of the waves can be heard clearly. The image of the man walks without pausing until the waters reach his head. All that is left behind is the hat floating calmly on the indifferent sea.

Victor Stein smiled. He walked forward, turning back to his screen. He said, I called this lecture *The Future of Humans in a Post-Human World* because artificial intelligence is not sentimental – it is biased towards best possible outcomes. The human race is not a best possible outcome.

He likes the audience to interact with him. To ask questions. He opens up the floor.

One of the Muslim women in the Sophia hoodies raises her hand. The runner passes the microphone.

Professor Stein, as you know, the Hanson robot, Sophia, was awarded citizenship of Saudi Arabia in 2017. She has more rights than any Saudi woman. What does this tell us about artificial intelligence?

Nothing – said Professor Stein – it tells us a great deal about Saudi Arabia.

(Laughter in the hall but the woman persists.)

Will women be the first casualties of obsolescence in your brave new world?

On the contrary, said Professor Stein, AI need not replicate outmoded gender prejudices. If there is no biological male or female, then—

But the woman interrupts him – he hates that, but he contains his irritation.

What about sexbots? Pulsing vaginas that never say no?

A young man gets in on the act – Yeah, and you don't even have to buy them dinner!

74

There's more laughter. The young man turns round to the women and smiles a big, wide, practised non-sexist smile – Just kidding! Can I get you guys a Coke later?

Professor Stein senses he is losing the room. He holds up his hand to quell the micro-conversations bubbling around the hall.

He has natural authority – like a lion tamer.

He says, There is a substantial difference between low-to-medium grade robotics that deploy narrow-goal outcomes – and I would include a pulsating vagina in that – even if she can call you Big Boy in eight languages . . . (Laughter.)

I spot a shape in the rear row jumping up and down to speak, but Professor Stein ignores the shape, and continues, *Please listen* . . . a substantial difference between narrow-goal outcomes and true artificial intelligence; by which I mean machines that will learn to think for themselves.

He pauses to let his words take effect. So, if your concern is that ultimately, will women be replaced by robots, as in *The Stepford Wives*, a film I love, by the way, and especially the remake with Glenn Close – have you seen that? No? Well, you should . . . it has a happy ending (he's joking to take back control by getting everyone on the same side, but there's resistance) – then I would say—

Another woman stands up to interrupt him. I see the splash of anger on his face like he's caught in a head-light. He takes a step back. The woman looks familiar to me. She's attractive in a discontented kind of way, blonde hair escaping from her clip, a torn, expensive jacket.

She says, Professor Stein, you are the acceptable face of AI, but in fact the race to create what you call true artificial intelligence is a race run by autistic-spectrum white boys with poor emotional intelligence and frat-dorm social skills. In what way will *their* brave new world be gender neutral – or anything neutral?

I wouldn't call the Chinese autistic-spectrum white boys, says Professor Stein mildly.

She says, China is a chauvinist culture where men grow up learning to disparage women . . . they are the biggest manufacturers and the biggest consumers of sexbots.

(I can see the guy in the back waving his hand again.)

She says, We know already that machine learning is deeply sexist in outcomes. Amazon had to stop using machines to sift through job application CVs because the machines chose men over women time after time. There is nothing neutral about AI.

Professor Stein holds up his hand to pause her . . . I agree with what you are saying about the current state of machine learning. Yes, there are problems – but it is my view that such problems are temporary, and not systemic.

The woman won't back down. She holds on to the microphone and shouts at him: WHAT IS SO SMART ABOUT THE END OF THE HUMAN?

There is a spontaneous round of applause in the hall; even some of the (rational, logical, forward-investing) men-in-suits applaud.

Victor looks unhappy. He wouldn't call it unhappy; he would call it misunderstood. He waits. He isn't patient, but he knows how to wait, the way an actor or a politician knows how to wait to deliver a line. Then he does one of the things he does so well – heads out of the sciences and into the arts:

To name things wrongly is to add to the misfortune of the world.

His voice-recognition app writes up the quote on the screen behind him. We stare at it. It is beautiful, like an equation.

There's a pause.

He waits again till the students have stopped tweeting and the geeks have stopped trying to find it online. He waits like he's got all the time in the world – and I suppose – if he's right – he has, because before he's dead he'll be able to upload his brain. The rest of us, as the lecture session reaches its end, know that it's 8:30 p.m. on a Wednesday. *Are you hungry?* I see it flash on the phone in front of me.

Victor speaks slowly and clearly. His voice is warm, and slightly accented from the years he has spent working in the States.

He says, Let me start by repeating what I said at the beginning of my lecture (in other words, weren't you listening, goldfish brain?). It is not the Silicon Valley geeks who are perversely turning life as we know it into an algorithm – it is the biologists. It is from the natural sciences that the barrier between organic and inorganic is being dismantled.

The room is quiet now. He continues . . .

What is an algorithm? An algorithm is a series of steps for solving a recurring problem. A problem isn't a bad thing – it's more of a How Do I? A problem might be – my route to work every morning; it might be, I am a tree – so how do I transpire? So an algorithm is a data-processing plant. Frogs, potatoes, humans can be understood as *biological* data-processing plants – if you believe the biologists. Computers are non-biological data-processing plants.

If data is the input and the rest is processing, then humans aren't so special after all.

And is that so terrible a piece of knowledge? Perhaps it comes as a relief. We haven't been wonderful as Masters of the Universe, have we? Climate change, mass extinction of fauna and flora, destruction of habitat and wilderness, atmospheric pollution, failure to control population, extraordinary brutality, the daily stupidity of our childish feelings . . .

He pauses again, his handsome face serious and sincere; yes, I think he means what he is about to say:

If we are reaching the end of Project Human, don't blame the geeks.

There is a loud cheer from the geeks in the room.

Victor continues, And science, remember, tries to deal in realities, not magical thinking. Science is no longer convinced that Homo sapiens is a special case.

Victor smiles and turns to his quote on the screen behind him:

To name things wrongly is to add to the misfortune of the world.

Albert Camus. You may not have read him, but perhaps you should. In any case, you all know, however vaguely, the Bible story of the Garden of Eden, and that Adam's task was to name his world. If you believe, as I do, that religious texts – like myths – are texts we create to mirror the deeper structures of the human psyche, then yes, naming is still our primary task. Poets and philosophers know this – perhaps science has confused naming with taxonomy. Perhaps, in our early efforts to distance ourselves from the alchemists who came before us, we forgot that naming is power. I cannot conjure spirits, but I can tell you that calling things by their right names is more than giving them an identity bracelet or a label, or a serial number. We summon a vision. Naming is power.

He comes forward to the front of the platform, the toes of his boots right on the edge, and he says, The world I imagine, the world that AI will make possible, will not be a world of labels – and that includes binaries like male and female, black and white, rich and poor. There will not be a division between head and heart, between what

I feel and what I think. The future will not be a version of *Blade Runner*, where replicants long to be named – like humans – and therefore to be known – like humans. What I am proposing is far bigger. As we develop true artificial intelligence, what are we doing? We are summoning a vision.

(He steps back. Pause. Wait. Hold. Go.)

Even if, even if the first superintelligence is the worst possible iteration of what you might call the white male autistic default programme, the first upgrade by the intelligence itself will begin to correct such errors. And why? Because we humans will only programme the future once. After that, the intelligence we create will manage itself.
    And us.
    Thank you.

APPLAUSE APPLAUSE APPLAUSE APPLAUSE.

The future is a plausible app.

I believe him. This second I truly do. Valhalla is burning and the white male gods are falling into the fire, but the Rheingold is what it always is – pure and untainted – and it will be found again, like a second chance, like a new beginning, and these will be the bad old days, when humans ruled the earth – which, by the way, will be restored as a nature reserve because AI won't need shopping malls and automobiles to satisfy its desires. All your worries about robots taking over your jobs – *dude, you can't even imagine the coming world . . .*

I didn't say that – it was a tweet.

There's a drinks reception afterwards. We can admire the portraits of Isaac Newton, Hook, Boyle, Franklin, Darwin, Faraday, Watson and Crick (apologies to Rosalind Franklin – the woman who supplied Watson and Crick with the vital X-rays they needed to unravel the structure of DNA).

Here's Tim Berners-Lee, Stephen Hawking, Venki Ramakrishnan. All the big guns, and only one female member of the Society has ever won a Nobel Prize (Dorothy Hodgkin). Maybe the next one will be a citizen of Saudi Arabia called Sophia.

The women in the hoodies are asking Victor if he has ever met Sophia, the Hanson robot with a sense of humour ('I want to kill all humans'). He has. He likes her. She is the reassuring face of robotics. It's all about humans and robots working together for a better life.

I know that Victor isn't really interested in robotics – he wants pure intelligence. But he sees robots as an intermediate species that will help humanity adjust to its coming role. The nature of that role is unclear.

In theory, if you own your own robot, you can send it out to work for you and keep the money. Or you can use it at home as an unpaid servant. Or you can send it to weed your chemical-free farm. Should be great. But when have things ever worked out great? In the human dream?

In the human dream.

Outside the window a cat walks along the parapet.

Hair falling over her shoulders, soft silk shirt under her leather jacket, the woman who wouldn't let go of the microphone is shoving her way towards Victor. She's feline, dangerous, part-wild, part-tame, like a zoo cat that can read and write.

Then she sees me. Jesus! she says. It's Dr Jackoff!

Yes, it's her. Polly D, Miss VIP.

How did your teledildonics work out? I say.

Just who or what are you? she asks. She presses her iPhone to RECORD.

The same now as I was then. And I am a medical doctor. Look!

I flip my ID at her. Now she's uncomfortable.

Then she sees Victor coming towards me. She gets on-message. Professor Stein! My name is Polly D. I work for *Vanity Fair* and I have been emailing you for some time. No reply. Why is that? I'd like to ask you a few questions.

This is not the moment, says Victor. The lecture is on the website, and you can email me via the link.

I have a few questions, insists Polly D.

Excuse me, please, says Victor. I have guests to attend to this evening. Ry!

*

82

Victor claps me on the back. I smile at Polly and shrug. I am a little bit pleased. Then I stop being pleased because I am obviously caught in one of those dreams where incongruous and mismatched people huddle in the same place. There he is . . . As large as his life.

You've met Ron Lord, haven't you, Ry?

Crumpled grey linen suit – faint urine stain on the crotch – I suppose it is urine – and a pink shirt that gapes between the fifth and sixth buttons. He's pink underneath too. TMI.

Ron is regarding me; reluctantly he holds out his hand. Well, good to see you again, Ryan.

It's Ry. Just Ry.

Not short for Ryan?

Ry is short for Mary.

Ron falls silent while he processes this fact. The thing about humans is that we process information at different speeds, depending on the human, depending on the information. In some ways machines are easier to deal with. If I had just told machine intelligence that I am now a man, although I was born a woman, it wouldn't slow up its processing speed.

You're a woman, then? says Ron.

No, Ron. I am a hybrid. My name is Ry.

You're a bloke, then? says Ron.

I'm trans.

Like, transhuman?

Transgender.

You look like a bloke, says Ron. Not a serious bloke, but a bloke. I wouldn't have given you that interview at the Sexpo if you was a girl.

I'm trans, I say again.

Victor has his hand on Ron's shoulder.

Ron has decided to become an investor, says Victor, in Optimal.

Optimal is Victor's company.

Optimal's logo reads: **The Future Is Now.** That annoys me because if the future is now, where is the present?

I reckon the prof and me are in the same business, says Ron.

You do? I say, looking at Victor.

Yeah, says Ron. The Future.

Victor is smiling. Not always a good sign. Ron, did you bring Claire?

Yeah! She's in the cloakroom folded in half. She's only about 2 foot 6 doubled up. I put her in a gym bag. There's a few of them in there – gym bags, I mean. Mine's the one that says ADIDAS.

I think some of our guests would like to see her, says Victor. She's reassuring.

Ron is not so reassured. I didn't like what you said about sexbots. About them being no threat. Every new development is a threat. Right? Some day robots will be an independent life form. That's what you told me when I said I might invest in you.

That is correct, says Victor. But at present all sexbots are narrow-goal robots.

You mean they got small cunts? says Ron.

That's not what I meant, says Victor.

So what exactly did you mean? says Ron. Mean? Exactly?

What I mean, says Victor, is that your robots do what it says on the box. They are for sex and personal satisfaction.

That's not a narrow goal, says Ron, that's the sum total. That's what men want.

Not all men, says Victor.

It's not what I want, I say, and Ron looks at me with even more doubt and even more dismay. He puts his free hand back in his pocket and waves his whisky glass at me. Listen, Ryan, or Mary, or whatever your name is, I'm not being personal, but have you got a dick?

I think that's personal, says Victor.

No, I say. My name is Ry and I don't have a dick.

Well then, says Ron, OK, no dick. So you're not a bloke really. So what blokes want – well, it's not about you, is it?

Is manhood dickhood? I ask Ron.

He looks at me like I am the stupidest thing he has ever seen. He says, Why would you want to be a man if you don't want a dick?

A man is not a dick on legs, is he?

More or less, says Ron.

There's a bit more to it, says Victor.

I am not sure how to proceed, so I keep it personal, and I say to Ron, *I didn't feel comfortable as a woman.*

Why not?

It's hard to explain.

Did you fancy women? You fancied women but you didn't fancy being a lesbian? I get that.

I am attracted to men, I say.

Ron takes a step back. His hand moves protectively towards his crotch. I want to say, *Don't worry, Ron, I don't mean you.*

Someone distracts Victor and I am left with nonplussed Ron. He says, Well, Ryan, I don't know if you're a bloke or whatever, but you are definitely a doctor, yeah?

That's right.

In a hospital?

Yes.

How do you know the prof?

I supply him with body parts.

Ron's pink nose starts twitching like a terrier's. Does he expect me to smell of mould? Is he looking for bloodstains? Dirt under my fingernails?

I'm not a *grave robber*, Ron. Do you think I go to the churchyard at night with a crowbar and a sack? You think I spade away the heaped mound of earth, prise open the coffin lid, lift her out from her last resting place, clothes damp with decay, and carry her off for dissection?

No! No! says Ron, meaning, Yes! Yes!

After dissection, in the old days, the human remains might be ground up as bonemeal, or rendered into candles, or fed to the pigs. There was no waste. You could say that burial is a waste – at least the way it's done these days, in solid caskets, worm-proof, rain-proof, anything to stop the natural processes of death.

Death is natural. Yet nothing looks more unnatural than a dead body.

It looks wrong, doesn't it, Ry? I remember when we first met, Victor's soft, urgent voice standing behind me. It looks wrong because it is wrong.

Victor Stein works across the boundary of smart medicine and machine learning. He is teaching non-human intelligence to diagnose. Machines are better than we are at the algorithms of disease. The doctor of the future will be a robot. But skin is skin, and flesh is flesh, and you can't learn anatomy from textbooks and videos. As long as there are bodies you will need a body. Body parts. I've seen the little probes gliding curiously across the muscles of a severed arm (preserved) and into the soft tissue of a leg (decaying). When you amputate a leg it has to be carried out of theatre. Legs are surprisingly heavy.

You amputate legs? says Ron.

Not only legs, I say.

How's it done? says Ron.

With a saw . . .

Ron looks paler now.

Then we cauterise the sliced end, wash and dry the discarded limb, drop it into a large plastic bag, seal it, label it and put it in the fridge or the freezer – or the incinerator – depending.

Depending, repeats Ron.

On its future. Not all severed legs have a future.

87

Do you know in advance? asks Ron.

Usually yes, but sometimes we have to amputate unexpectedly. And it depends how much of the leg we need to remove . . . and whether the patient will be able to use a prosthetic. You should discuss prosthetics with Professor Stein. Transhuman enhancement may begin with computer controlled prosthetic limbs.

I like my legs, says Ron, looking down. They're not fast, and they are both fat, but I've had them a long time.

I understand, I say.

There is a pause while Ron contemplates his legs. He asks me, with the childlike trust people put in doctors, How much does my leg weigh?

Ron's legs are short but substantial. I take a guess: Around twenty kilos, detached here . . . I run my finger at groin level. He dresses on the left.

Ron jumps, and looks down apprehensively at the crumpled cloth of his still attached lower limb.

What big hands you've got, he says.

All the better to amputate you with.

Ron steps back.

Have you considered donating your body to science, Ron? I ask.

You've got a bloke's hands, says Ron.

I do have big hands, it's true. My mother had big hands. She died giving birth to me, but in the photographs I have of her she's strong and clear-eyed and unafraid. Can you miss someone you never knew? I miss her.

I am not especially tall at 5 foot 8. My build is slender. Narrow hips, long legs. When I had top surgery there wasn't much to remove, and the hormones had already altered my chest. I never wore a bra when I was female. I like my chest the way it is now; strong, smooth and flat. I wear my hair tied back in a ponytail like an eighteenth-century poet. When I look in the mirror I see someone I recognise, or rather, I see at least two people I recognise. That is why I have chosen not to have lower surgery. I am what I am, but what I am is not one thing, not one gender. I live with doubleness.

Victor comes back over with another glass of whisky for Ron.

You two seem to be getting on well, he says, looking at me quizzically, in the way that he does.

I was telling Ron about your body parts, I said. I was explaining to him about our special relationship.

Ah, yes, said Victor. Every lab needs its body parts. Now he's looking at me anxiously: how much have I said? Too bad. Let him sweat. Like Ron Lord.

What I didn't say to Ron is that Victor Stein needs more body parts than his research allowance allows.

Just then two security guards in blue shirts come running through the room pulling on gloves and waving their Tasers. STAND BACK STAND BACK STAND BACK!

Victor follows the guards and I follow Victor as they run towards the cloakroom. The cloakroom attendant is looking pale.

It's in there! she says. It's alive! It moved! There's an animal in that bag.

The guard moves towards the Adidas gym bag. He leans down. *Blimey! I can hear something talking!*

His colleague bends over the bag. He's sceptical.

He says, You fancy yourself as Doctor Dolittle? Give it a prod!

He prods the bag. Nothing happens.

By now there is a crowd at the cloakroom. The guard stands on a chair. Is anyone responsible for an Adidas gym bag?

Ron Lord's pink hand appears above the crowd-line.

That's my bag!

Open it up, please, sir! says the guard.

I can see Polly D standing on a chair, videoing this with her phone.

Ron shoulders his way through the crowd like he's his own bouncer at his own nightclub. He picks up the bag, lays it on the cloakroom counter and unzips it. Out comes a sex-doll, folded in half. Her denim jacket has CLAIRE written on it in sequins.

DADDY! says Claire.

I don't know how she got set off, says Ron. She's controlled by an app.

What is this thing? asks the security guard.

She's a sexbot, says Ron. The prof asked me to bring her to the talk. In case anybody wanted to see one. Wait a sec. She needs unfolding.

Ron pulls down Claire's legs one at a time.

OPEN MY LEGS, DADDY! WIDER!

Embarrassed giggles, horrors, OMGs, Yikes, This cannot be for real, Yuck, Cool, Let me see that!

Her legs unfolded, Ron stands Claire up, holding her from behind like a ventriloquist. Claire is wearing a pair of shorts and a tight crop-top with a black bra underneath. Ron adjusts her hair.

This is her travelling outfit, he says. You can't fold up the legs in a skirt without splitting it.

SPLIT ME! says Claire.

Sorry about this, says Ron, Claire is sexually explicit if she is in Bedroom Mode.

He reaches into his pocket for his phone. He says, I can go into the app and put her into Visitor Mode. Wait . . .

DON'T MAKE ME WAIT, DADDY!

I can't get a signal down here, says Ron.

I TOUCH MYSELF DOWN HERE!

Claire is like a parrot on heat. Her programming allows her to pick up and repeat words. Ron is holding his phone above his head. He says, Can somebody grab Claire while I sort out my fuckin' phone?

Ron thrusts Claire at one of the women standing near by.

The woman can't believe she's holding a sex-doll.

Turn it this way! Towards me! shouts Polly D from on top of her chair.

Oh my God! says the woman. She's got, like, a 20-inch waist and 40-inch boobs.

BOOBS. NIPPLES. COCK, says Claire.

Awesome! says a geek boy.

What's this bracket in her back? asks one of the guys, examining Claire.

That's an optional extra, says Ron. She can be wall-mounted.

Like a trophy on the wall? says one of the women.

No! says Ron. So that you can fuck her standing up.

FUCK ME STANDING UP, DADDY.

That is gross! shouts Polly D.

Ron shrugs. Suit yourself . . .

Some of the boys are enjoying this; I can tell from the rise in their jeans. Ron is sweating visibly as his fat fingers work his iPhone.

HOW WAS YOUR JOURNEY TODAY? says Claire.

Thank God for that! says Ron. She's in Visitor Mode now. I realise this place is a serious scientific institution.

HAVE YOU COME FROM AN INSTITUTION?

Just let me explain, says Ron, that Claire is a sex-therapy aid. This model isn't sophisticated, but she will do what you tell her.

(Sniggers from the crowd crowding round.)

Here, says Ron, let me show you. Put your finger in her mouth. Go on.

One of the men hesitates but he does it. He jumps back like he's been bitten. That's weird!

Vibrates, right? says Ron, beaming. And that's just your finger. And that's just her mouth.

(Laughter.)

What's the point of this? I say to Victor. Why are you encouraging him?

Victor shrugs. This is the coming world. When people have nothing to do all day they will have time for a lot more sex.

That isn't sex, Victor.

I can't decide with you, Ry, whether you are a Puritan or a Romantic.

I am a human being.

And what if you were one of the millions of human beings who will have no place in the automated life that will soon be reality? Cars, trucks, buses, trains will drive themselves. Stores and supermarkets will use smart tracking for your purchases. Your home will use repair diagnostics. Your fridge will order its own food. Bots will take care of the housework and entertain your children. What will you do all day?

That's not how you sold it in your lecture.

And that is not how it will be for those of us able to be part of the new world. For us, life will be unlimited.

DO YOU ENJOY YOUR JOB? says Claire.

For the rest, says Victor, there must be diversions and soporifics. Sex-dolls can provide both.

Not for women, it seems, I said as we looked across at the crowd, now shaped into two groups, male and female, the men laughing and joking with Ron, the women talking to each other in low voices of despair or disbelief.

I agree, says Victor. Women are harder to please.

Polly D looks pretty pleased with herself at this moment. She jumps off the chair and skirts the crowd to leave.

She's on to you, Victor, I tell him.

There's nothing to worry about, he says. I've seen her before. She's a journalist, that's all.

And what about Ron Lord? I ask him. Why do you want his money?

Victor shrugs. Why not? He is a maverick, an outsider. He wants results. There are things I want to do . . .

What kind of things?

We are at an interesting moment . . . says Victor.

Ron Lord comes over. He thinks he is a success.

They love her! he says. Once they get to know her, yeah, they all love her. Tell you what – I'll take us all out for something to eat. Prof! Ryan? I could murder a steak.

Good job it's already dead, I say.

Ron looks at me more in sorrow than in anger.

Ryan, I am extending the hand, he says.

Thanks, Ron, but I'm vegetarian.

I knew you wasn't a bloke, says Ron.

Ry! Come with us. We can walk up to Sheekey's. You can have vegetarian fish.

Ron turns to retrieve Claire from her admirers.

Victor says to me, Will I see you later?

Do you want to see me later?

I want to see you now and later.

I'll call you, I said.

Ron returned with his Adidas bag full of Claire.

I raise my (big) hand to signal goodbye. Going, going, gone.

Outside on The Mall, the buildings are blurred with light rain. My boot cleats leave prints on the cellophane smoothness of the wet pavements. I look back – there's a trace of me, and then the prints disappear under the rain. On the road, cars queue in tail-light red. Horns. Traffic noise. Ceaseless. Comforting. The rain increases. On the street, under hoods and umbrellas, people are walking quickly, going somewhere, leaving somewhere, earphones in, their faces lit by phone-light, atomised and alone.

I am alone.

Am I alone?

There is always something to break the solipsism.

She falls into step with me. Polly D.

Look, I was rude. I am sorry. Can I get you a drink?

Sure, I say; where do you want to go?

I'm a member of a club – not far – 2 Brydges Place. Just the other side of Trafalgar Square.

And soon we're sitting in a tiny wood-panelled room in a maze of tiny wood-panelled rooms, some with open fires. The year could be 1816. Polly D gets wine in a decanter and asks for a plate of bread and cheese. She says, I love this place. I like anything that sits across time. Makes me feel free.

It might be a little phony, I said. Maybe a little too theme-park? Welcome to the 1800s?

We're all here as something we're not, aren't we? she said. Playing a role of some kind.

(I don't answer. I look at her suede boots with fringes.)

I overheard, she said. You're trans . . .

Yes.

It's a good look.

It's not a look; it's who I am. Both of me. All of me.

I get it. I get it. (But she would say that.) Then she says, Do you prefer women or men? As partners?

I have had both. I seem to prefer men.

For sex?

Yes, for sex.

Was it like that when you were fully female?

I said, I am fully female. I am also partly male. That's how it is for me. But to answer your question – I was in a relationship with a woman for a while. It didn't work out.

The love or the sex?

The love.

(I don't want to talk about this.)

Maybe I could interview you? Trans is hot right now.

It's not a fashion choice, OK?

No, no, I mean, you, as a doctor . . . what was it like taking all that testosterone? Having the surgery? You could be an icon.

Polly, I'm not Caitlyn Jenner. I don't want to be in *Vanity Fair*.

Polly D looked genuinely confused. She said, Why not?

I sat in silence eating cheese. After several minutes of this, Polly recognised that she needed a new topic of conversation. She poured me more wine. She made eye contact.

So you know him? Victor Stein.

I know him. You seemed rather hostile tonight.

It's not that . . . (She undoes her hair, shakes it loose, leans forward.) I don't trust the way AI is being sold to us. People aren't in the conversation, let alone the decisions. We're going to wake up one morning and the world won't be the same.

That morning could be any morning, I say. It could be climate breakdown. It could be nuclear. It could be Trump or Bolsonaro. It could be *The Handmaid's Tale*.

That's just what I mean, she says. We think change is gradual, incremental, that we'll get used to it, adapt. But this feels different. And I hate the fuckin' sexbots!

You do? Intelligent Vibrators??? Teledildonics?

She laughed. When she laughs she looks calm, kind even.

She said, I had to test the sex aids and smart apps for women. It was crazy. You know you can get a personal sex-therapy app, like the friend you never had.

And probably never wanted, I said.

Do you have friends? she said.

Of course! Do you?

She didn't answer me. She said, So tell me about what you were doing in Memphis?

You can read the essay on the Wellcome Trust website.

Send me a link, she said. What's your mail?

I sent her the link. I said, The essay is about human relationships, mental health and the effect of bots on both of those things. I don't believe the effects will be necessarily negative, by the way.

Polly interrupted me (again). You don't think sexbots are negative?

Let me finish! It's not only sexbots. Children will soon have mini-iPals to keep them company – bots with computer screens in their chests. Bots that will sing to the kids. Tell them a story. Play games. Mother's little helper. Bots that—

Polly dived back in: That's just part of the sell, though, isn't it? To make us feel good? And what about the big one? The real AI?

We're nowhere near that yet.

How do you know?

Victor knows.

Do you like him?

Yes, I like him.

How did you two meet?

(Is this what she is really interested in?)

Why do you want to know?

I'm trying to profile him. It isn't easy. He's elusive.

I'm not the key to that door, I said.

Are you in love with him?

Do you say whatever comes into your head?

I just wondered . . . something about the way you were with him tonight.

Thanks for the drink, I said, getting up to leave.

The rain is heavy now. The streets are empty. My hospital isn't far from here. There's a painted sign in the Terminal Ward; one of the patients made it:

LOVE IS AS STRONG AS DEATH.
It's from the Bible. Song of Solomon.

Death is where I met him. The Alcor Life Extension Foundation. Phoenix. Arizona.

THE FUTURE IS NOW

This futuristic charnel house. This warehouse for the departed. This stainless-steel tomb. This liquid-nitrogen limbo. This down-payment plan eternity. This resin block of nothingness. This one-chance wonder. This polished morgue. This desert address. A nice town to live in. This sunset boulevard. Dead men. Not walking. Hotel Vitrification.

Alcor opened its doors in 1972 – the Chinese Year of the Rat. The ultimate survivor.

Should you decide to gamble on your resurrection here at the Casino for the Dead, this is what happens:

As soon as possible after death – and preferably the team is already assembled near by, masks on faces, discreetly waiting for your last breath – your body will be placed in a bath of ice water to lower its temperature down to around 60 degrees Fahrenheit. Blood circulation and lung function will be artificially restored using a heart – lung resuscitator. Not to revive you but to prevent your blood from pooling in your abdomen.

The medical team will access your major blood vessels and you will be connected to a perfusion machine that will remove your blood, and replace it with a chemical solution that prevents the formation of ice crystals in the cells of your body. You are going to be vitrified – not frozen. The process of filling you with cryoprotectant takes about four hours. Two small holes will be drilled in your skull so that brain perfusion can be observed.

Then you will be further cooled over the next three hours to make sure that your suspended body is like glass, not ice. After two weeks you are ready for your final resting place – at least in this life.

I came by invitation. An invitation to be part of the Field Team, a team of medics and paramedics who will preserve your body fast enough if you die too far away from Alcor.

(And most of us will . . .)

The invitation was a mistake. I am part of a small group of transgender medical professionals. Some of us are transhuman enthusiasts too. That isn't surprising; we feel or have felt that we're in the wrong body. We can understand the feeling that any-body is the wrong body.

Transhuman means different things to different people; smart implants, genetic modification, prosthetic enhancement, even the chance to live forever as a brain emulation.

So, out of ordinary semantic confusion – the kind that humans live with every day – came the invitation to be a White Knight of Life. The Black Knight is Death. Here I am, charging to the rescue. There isn't much time after the heart stops to halt the disintegration of the cells, systems, tissues of the body.

In some sense, if you are dedicated to the preservation of life, then you are, by definition, not dedicated to the inevitability of death. It is my job to extend life. Alcor hopes to extend life indefinitely.

Max More, the CEO and director of the facility, hoped I might be part of their international team – in my case, UK-based – as the future expanded. Max is British. He wants us to catch up with the future.

We call this place Alcor, he said, because that's the name of a 5th-magnitude star. You can see it if you have good eyesight, but it's in the distance, like the future.

One day, says Max, we'll live among the stars.

The only problem with cryonics is that no one knows how to reheat the body without destroying it. But, as Max points out, Leonardo da Vinci made drawings of helicopters centuries before powered flight.

The time will come, says Max. It always does.

He suggested I look around for myself, get a sense of the place.

So here I am in what looks like a giant stainless-steel warehouse. It's silent except for the hum of systems.

To protect privacy there are no names on the cylinders, but for one, far smaller than the rest, looking more like a cigar tube than a space-pod. It bears a label that reads: Dr James H. Bedford.

I learn that Bedford was the first human to be cryonically preserved back in 1967.

1969: astronauts went to the moon, Bedford had gone to inner space. He was a pioneer of cryonics. So much so that for a few years his family kept him in a self-storage lock-up and topped up the liquid nitrogen themselves.

He was recently removed to a more up-to-date container. The opening of the casket was emotional, like he was a modern-day mummy from old Memphis. Apparently his body was in excellent shape, apart from a chest fracture and a collapsed nose. That can be fixed when he returns.

I heard a voice behind me. It's a little like an art installation in here, isn't it? Have you seen Damian Hirst's pickled shark in a tank? What does he call it? *The Impossibility of Death in the Mind of Someone Living.*

I turned round. A man in his fifties, well-preserved. Botox for sure. Perhaps more if I could look for the scar-lines behind his ears. Tight skin, clean-shaven, dark, restless eyes. He held out his hand to greet me.

My name is Victor Stein.

I shook his hand. Ry Shelley.

He held on to my hand: Have we met?

And the strange, split-second other-world answer is *yes*.
No, I say.
He looks at me, nodding slightly.
How long are you here?
I leave in the morning. I'm a guest of Max.
Ah, yes. The English Doctor?
That's me. Do you work here?
No, no. I am here to see a friend. Call him the English
Patient.
He smiles. I smile. Then he says, Well, would you care
for a drink later? When you're done with your business?
There's a place I know . . .
I am in the process of saying no.
Yes, I say. Why not?

Time is a zip. Sometimes it snags.
And so, a few hours afterwards, when Max More had
gone home and there was nothing for me to do at my
motel except pack, eat a takeaway and watch terrible TV,
I got into Victor's rented SUV and we headed out of
town. Diners, gas stations, retail outlets, trucks going
somewhere, a broken-down Jeep going nowhere. Heat
on the windshield. A road stretching distance into
distance. Dust trails behind us.
We drove into the radiant emptiness of the Sonoran Desert.

Where are you from? he asks me.
Manchester.

That's funny.

What's funny about Manchester?

Nothing – well, maybe some things, only, my lab is there, at the university. It's privately funded but hosted by the University of Manchester.

I was born in Manchester. I don't live there now.

London?

Yes, London.

We're all global travellers, aren't we? We're all somewhere else. Did you know that there are thirty-six Manchesters in the world? Thirty-one of them in the USA?

That's the Industrial Revolution for you, I say.

In fact, he says, it was the Lancashire cotton workers' solidarity with Abraham Lincoln over slavery. Manchester workers refused to process cotton from the slave plantations. In those days, ninety-eight per cent of the world's cotton was processed in Manchester. Can you imagine that?

Times change, I said.

Yes, he said, many cotton workers, pressed by hardship, booked passage from Liverpool to the brave new world of America and took their Manchester with them. The future always carries something from the past.

Like humans, I said. Mitochondrial DNA.

He nodded. Men don't carry it, do they?

I said, Men carry it but they can't pass it on. Only the mother passes it on, right back to the mother of us all.

He said 200,000 years ago in Africa. The first humans. Think how long it took us to reach the Industrial Revolution. And think how far and how fast we've travelled in the last 200 years.

Are you having your body preserved? I ask him.

Certainly not! You?

No!

It's old-fashioned. No one will want their diseased body back. The brain, though – well . . . And that's where they're heading now – pardon the pun – I am sure Max told you? You saw this on their website? Victor passes me his phone.

Cryopreservation that is focused on doing the best possible job to preserve the human brain is called 'neuro-preservation.' The brain is a fragile organ that cannot be removed from the skull without injury, so it is left within the skull during preservation and storage for good ethical and scientific reasons. This gives rise to the mistaken impression that Alcor preserves 'heads'. It is more accurate to say that Alcor preserves brains in the least injurious way possible.

Do you really think a brain can be brought back to functioning consciousness? I say.

Probably, he says.

His hands on the wheel are long, well-kept and clean. I notice hands. I am a surgeon. He wears a gold signet ring on his little finger.

He swings the wheel and pulls the car into a dirt lot. I see a shack with a tin roof and a covered walkway to beat off the sun. Cacti. Jack rabbits. Wooden tables outside. Swivel stools at the bar. Pretty waitress wearing an Eagles T-shirt. TAKE IT EASY. Four Roses Bourbon on the rocks. Toasted cheese. Haze of sunset. Big birds flying across the sky.

Of course, says Victor, what I would prefer is to be able to upload myself, that is, upload my consciousness, to a substrate not made of meat. At present, though, that is not an effective way to prolong life because the operation to scan and copy the contents of my brain will kill me.

Isn't content also context? I ask him. Your experiences, your circumstances, the time you live in? Consciousness isn't free-floating; it's enmeshed.

That is true, he says, but you know, I believe that the modern diaspora – that so many of us find ourselves somewhere else, migrants of some kind – global, multicultural, less rooted, less dependent on our immediate history of family or country to shape ourselves – all of that is preparing us for a looser and freer understanding of ourselves as content whose context can change.

Nationalism is on the rise, I say.

He nods. That is a throwback. A fear. A refusal of the future. But the future cannot be refused.

I ask him what he does. His speciality is machine learning and human augmentation. A first degree in Computer Science from Cambridge. A PhD on computer learning from Virginia Tech called *Do Robots Read?* Impressive stints in robotic engineering at Lockheed, then a mysterious time at DARPA, the Defense Advanced Research Projects Agency based in Virginia. DARPA is a federal government agency, lavishly funded, that works on military tech, including unmanned drones and killer-bots. Now he's an advisor to Railes Prosthetics on how 'smart' artificial limbs might become integrated body parts.

But his day-to-day work, he says, is in his lab teaching machines how to diagnose the human condition.

Good luck, I say. I have no idea how to diagnose the human condition, much less how to cure it.

End death, said Victor.

That's impossible.

It is only impossible for biological organisms.

The waitress comes over. Short skirt. Wide smile. She catches me looking at her TAKE IT EASY T-shirt and misinterprets my interest. She doesn't seem to mind; I guess she's used to it. She turns round. On the back there's a line from the song: *We may lose and we may win though we will never be here again.*

That's kinda sad, isn't it? she said.

Would you like to live forever? Victor asked her.

Forever is too long, she said. I'd like to look good and be healthy. Maybe live to a hundred looking twenty-five.

How would you feel about dying if you reached a hundred and looked twenty-five? asked Victor.

The waitress considered this question carefully. Maybe we could be programmed to end? she said. Like the replicants in *Blade Runner.*

That will be hard – when the moment comes, said Victor. The replicants didn't like it.

I think I could manage hard, said the waitress. I am managing right now. I have a kid. I work this job and I am a hair stylist too. Life is hard. Hard is OK. It's hopeless and helpless that sucks.

Do you believe her? said Victor, when she had gone to lean over another table.

I believe she believes herself. That's different.

Victor nodded. He said, Tell me this, Ry, if you were certain that by disrupting everything you take for granted about the mind, about the body, about biology, about death, about life, if you were certain that such a disruption would bring about a personal, social, global utopia, would you risk it?

(He's crazy, I thought.)

Yes, I said.

He poured us more bourbon from the bottle. What's the future of alcohol? I said.

He raised his glass. As I said, the future always brings something from the past.

I have a sense he drinks heavily. But there's no paunch, no redness, no sag. He looks like a macrobiotic fitness freak on cucumber water. He downs his whisky. He hasn't touched the toasted cheese. I decide to finish his. He can tell what I'm thinking: he says, I don't mix protein and carbs. We can get a steak here later.

I'm leaving first thing in the morning.

Then as you are not leaving tonight we could have dinner.

It is easy to be controlled by someone who is controlling and charming. And, outside of my job, I

112

dislike decisions. I'll go with the flow on this – in any case, I've just spent the day at a recycling centre for dead bodies. Food, drink and a madman are a good distraction.

I get the sense, deep down, that Victor Stein is a high-functioning madman.

He says, You've heard of Alan Turing, of course?

I'm nodding. Hasn't everyone? Breaking the Code. Bletchley Park. Benedict Cumberbatch playing a suitably autistic computer genius.

Then, said Victor Stein, I wonder if you know that when Turing first used the word, the term, *computer* he wasn't referring to a machine at all – but to a person. The person would be the computer . . . admittedly the person would be analysing machine-generated data – but unconsciously, perhaps, when he thought of a computer as a person he had a futuristic sense of where we would travel.

Where are we travelling? I said.

That depends on whose story you believe, said Victor. Or whose story you want to believe. It's always a story, you know.

What are my options? I said.

Well, in no particular order, said Victor, options are as follows: humans will learn how to halt and reverse the ageing process; we will all live healthier and longer lives. We're still biology but we're better biology. Alongside that, we can enhance ourselves with smart implants to improve our physical and mental capacities.

Alternatively, because biology is limited, we abolish death, at least for some people, by uploading our minds out of their biological beginnings.

I interrupted him, But then we're just a computer programme.

He frowned. Why do you say 'just'? Do you think that Stephen Hawking, whose body was useless to him, was 'just' a mind? He was a mind, certainly, and the closest thing we have seen to an exceptional and fully conscious human mind trapped in a body. What if we had been able to free his mind? What would he have chosen, do you think?

But he began in a functioning body.

And so will any mind that is uploaded – and that brings me to my third option.

I decide to shut up and let him talk.

He smiles at me. He has a questioning smile. Part invitation, part challenge.

He says, At the same time as all or any of those possibilities, we also create various kinds of artificial intelligence, from robots to supercomputers, and we learn to live with newly created life forms. Life forms that might, eventually, phase out the bio-element altogether.

Or we could just go on as we are, I said.

He shook his head. Of the scenarios I have sketched, your alternative is the only one that is impossible.

The waitress came over with our check. There's a storm coming, she said.

*

Victor Stein suggested we leave the SUV in the parking lot and walk a while, before returning to eat that steak.

I like to walk before dinner, he said.

How are you going to manage that when you're just an upload? I asked.

I won't be eating dinner, he said.

He was laughing. Once out of the body you will be able to choose any form you like, and change it as often as you like. Animal, vegetable, mineral. The gods appeared in human form and animal form, and they changed others into trees or birds. Those were stories about the future. We have always known that we are not limited to the shape we inhabit.

What is reality? I said. To you?

It's not a noun, said Victor. It's not a thing or an object. It isn't objective.

I said, I accept that our experience of reality isn't objective. My subjective experience of the desert will be different to yours, but the desert is really there.

The Buddha would not agree with you, said Victor. The Buddha would argue that you are a slave to appearances, that you confuse reality with appearance.

Then what is reality?

The best minds have asked this question forever, said Victor. I cannot answer it. What I can say is that just as consciousness appears to be an emergent property of brain function – you can't pinpoint consciousness biologically – it is as elusive as the seat of the soul – but we would agree that consciousness exists – and we would agree that at present machine intelligence isn't conscious. So perhaps reality is also an emergent property – it exists, but it is not the material fact we take it to be.

In front of me I watched the material fact of a pocket mouse racing towards a creosote bush. We heard the storm before we felt it. The deep crash of thunder. Then the forked lightning above our heads.

And then it rained.

The Sonoran Desert is one of the wettest deserts in North America. It has two rainy seasons – this was the summer season – heavy and sudden.

This won't last long! shouted Victor above the smash of thunder. This is a BWh climate. Dry, arid, hot.

I said, Makes no difference how you classify it; we're soaked.

And we were. As if buckets of water had been poured over our heads. Victor's blue linen shirt clung to his body. My T-shirt hung loose and dripping.

Victor took a handkerchief out of his pocket and wiped his face. Who carries a handkerchief?

There's an overhang! We can shelter under that rock!

We ran towards it. There was barely room for us both. I was conscious of his body, a warm, wet animal, next to me. I lifted my T-shirt to rub my eyes, feeling the stream of rain down my stomach. When I looked up, Victor was staring at me.

You're shivering, he said. It's not cold but you are shivering.

116

A thunderclap dislodged small pieces of rock above us. Victor put his hand on my shoulder. I think we had better go, he said.

We walked in silence. Nature can cancel thought. We needed to walk and there was nothing more to say.

Out on the porch of the bar under the clatter of rain on the tin roof I could see our waitress waiting for us.

You boys need somewhere to take a shower and dry off? There's a room out the back. I can wash and dry those clothes if you want. Won't take an hour.

Where does kindness come from? I said to Victor.

Evolutionary cooperation, he said. Competition alone would have wiped us out.

Can you programme kindness?

Yes, he said.

We stood on the porch, stripping down to our boxer shorts. His were blue to match his trousers. Mine were orange.

Cute, said the waitress; you can throw those into this basket when you get inside.

Do you do this for all your customers? said Victor.

Most of 'em don't go walking in the desert when I say there's a storm coming. Now go on in and I'll bring you both a whisky.

The room was dark. The window was dusty with sand behind a half-closed shutter. There was a bed, a couple of chairs, a battered TV and a wardrobe. The shower room was white-tiled and basic.

You first, said Victor. Throw me your shorts and I'll put them in the basket. She's waiting.

I went into the bathroom and tossed my shorts through the door. I heard Victor turn on the TV to the weather channel.

The shower was plentiful and strong and the water was hot. I soaped my body, getting rid of sand from every crack and soft place. Soon the room was as steamy as a Hitchcock movie. I didn't notice Victor had come in until I stepped out of the shower. He handed me a towel. Then he saw me.

He saw the scars under my pecs. I watched his eyes work down my body. No penis.

There was a pause, short enough but long enough.

I'm trans, I said. I had top surgery about a year ago. These things take time.

I am slender. Lightly built with broad shoulders. When I was entirely a woman I was sometimes mistaken for a boy if I tied back my hair. I wore it shoulder-length as a woman. Now it is a little shorter but I still wear it tied back. Women like it. They like me.

Victor said nothing. Strange and touching in a fluent person. I stood still and let him look at me. My pubic hair is abundant but my body is smooth and not hairy. That didn't change with the testosterone.

118

I looked at him too. The hair on his chest and the line of it down his stomach.

Your chest hair is full of sand, I said. I moved closer. I brushed it away. I saw him swallow. He took my towel from me and wrapped it around his waist.

I thought you were a man, he said.

I am. Anatomically I am also a woman.

Is that how you feel about yourself?

Yes. Doubleness is nearer to the truth for me.

Victor said, I have never met anyone who is trans.

Most people haven't.

He smiled. Weren't we just saying that in the future we will be able to choose our bodies? And to change them? Think of yourself as future-early.

I am always late for appointments, I said, and we both laughed. To break the tension.

Once you are out of the room I will drop this towel and take a shower.

The thin towel wasn't hiding much. I said (why did I say this?), Do you want to touch me?

I'm not gay, he said.

I know it's confusing, I said.

He moved nearer. He ran his long fingers down my forehead and over my nose, parted my lips and rubbed my two front teeth, pulled down my lower lip, passed on over the light stubble of my chin and to my non-existent Adam's apple, the dip of my throat, then he spread his hand, thumb and fingers on either side of my collarbone. As though he was scanning me.

With his other hand, flat, he stroked my chest, pausing over the scars. He is not afraid of the scars or their bumpy beauty. To me they are beautiful. A mark of freedom. When I find them in the night, in the dark, I remember what I have done, and I go back to sleep.

He touched my nipples. My nipples have always been sensitive, now more so since the surgery. My chest is strong and smooth from the weight training I do. The testosterone injections make it easy to build muscle. I like the solid plane of what I have become. We were near to kissing but we didn't kiss.

Gently he turned me round, facing away from him. His front to my back. His breath on my neck. His hands exploring the same parts of me: chest, nipples, throat. I could feel his erection under the rough, thin cotton towel.

He kissed my shoulders, leaning down. He is taller than me. Gentle kisses, the kind given on the top of the head. Then, pressing himself closer against my body, he moved his hand between my legs and began to massage me.

You're wet, he said.

His finger was inside me.

This is . . .

As it always was, I said.

And this?

The clitoris gets much bigger with testosterone.

Is it sensitive?

I have 8,000 nerves in my clitoris. Your penis gets by on 4,000. Yes, it is sensitive.

He took it between his finger and thumb, his middle finger inside me.

Every clitoris gets erect but when you have one 2 inches long it's obvious.

Wait . . .

I turned to face him. I unknotted his towel and took his penis in my hand, kissing him. I could feel him pulsing.

What do you want me to do? he said.

What do you want to do?

Fuck you.

We went back into the room. He lay down on his back and pulled me onto him, moving my hips to slide me across his penis for maximum pleasure for me. I come faster than I used to as a woman, and I was excited with the kind of excitement that happens with a stranger.

I'm coming, I said.

I watched his eyes, dark, mesmerised, the glowing part of him.

I fell forward in the throb of it, my body on top of his. He spun me over and went inside me, his forearms on either side of my shoulders, his head in my neck.

He was done in about three minutes.

We lay looking at the ceiling. Not speaking. The rain rattled the shutters. I leaned up on my elbow and looked at his face.

I said, Are you OK?

You don't have to look after me just because you were once a woman, he said.

I am a woman. And I am a man. That's how it is for me. I am in the body that I prefer. But the past, my past, isn't subject to surgery. I didn't do it to distance myself from myself. I did it to get nearer to myself.

He rolled over. I don't know what to say, he said.

What do you feel? I said.

Incredibly aroused.

He took my hand to touch him again.

I sat on him.

It was slower this time. As he moved inside me, I touched myself, pulling my clit towards its pleasure. He watched me.

Why are you so easy in your body? he said.

Because it really is my body. I had it made for me.

He smiled. Oh, God . . .

What's the matter?

What's going to happen? he said.

What do you mean?

I'm a Bayesian.

Is that a religious cult?

No! Didn't you have to take Maths to be a doctor?

Physics, Chemistry, Biology . . .

All right, well, the Reverend Thomas Bayes 1701–1761 was a mathematician and a philosopher. He worked out equations to manage probability. His view was that subjective belief should change to accommodate available evidence. He wrote a powerful piece- called *An Essay Towards Solving a Problem in the Doctrine of Chances*. It's mathematics meets mysticism. Most people only concern themselves with the maths . . . But never mind that. What I am calculating is that you are a very unlikely chance in my life – zero probability – but you have occurred. And the thing about probability is that new data continuously alters the outcome.

I slide off his dick. Is that what I am? New data?

He kissed me. Delicious new data, but you will affect the outcome.

What outcome?

Outside we heard the waitress calling.

You boys! Y'all right in there?

Methinks, wrote Byron to the publisher John Murray, it is a wonderful work for a girl of nineteen – *not* nineteen, indeed, at that time.

You must create a female for me, with whom I can live in the interchange of those sympathies necessary for my being . . . I demand a creature of another sex, but as hideous as myself . . . It is true we shall be monsters, cut off from all the world; but on that account we shall be more attached to one another. Our lives will not be happy, but they will be harmless, and free from misery I now feel.

If you consent, neither you nor any other human being shall ever see us again: I will go to the vast wilds of South America . . . My life will flow quietly away, and, in my dying moments, I shall not curse my maker.

My husband is out on the lake with Byron. The house is still and hot. As the house dries it steams, and seems filled with apparitions, as our minds shape the steam into forms we fancy we recognise.

What do we recognise? What do we know?

In the progress of my story I am educating my monster. My monster is educating me.

The progress of my story forces me to question what such a being might desire. Might such a being long for a mate? Could such a being reproduce? And would the

127

progeny be ghastly and deformed? Or human? And if not human, then what life form would a life form such as this recreate?

I feel the like agony of mind of Victor Frankenstein; having created his monster, he cannot uncreate him. Time has no pity. Time cannot unhappen. What is done is done.

And so it is that I have created my monster and his master. My story has being. I must continue it, for it cannot end without me.

The monster I have made is shunned and feared by humankind. His difference is his downfall. He claims no natural home. He is not human, yet the sum of all he has learned is from humankind.

Last night I sat up late with Shelley. He had removed his clothes but for his shirt. The whiteness of him glistened in the moonlight. The male body is the perfect form, I believe. And such is the travesty of my monster. In proportion but monstrous.

I ran my hand along Shelley's leg from ankle to the top of his thigh, disturbing the folds of his shirt and his concentration. Gently he removed my hand, reserving his pleasure. *I am thinking,* he said.

We wondered together about the title for my story. We agreed that it should not contain the word MONSTER.

I have a hum in my head of a line from a poem of his that I love: *Alastor; or, the Spirit of Solitude.* He recites to me, standing up, pacing the room, his legs seem like wings, they propel him at such speed. Wings below the waist? What kind of an angel would he be, my angel?

Listen to him:

In lone and silent hours
When night makes a weird sound of its own stillness
Like an inspired and desperate alcymist
Staking his very life on some dark hope,
Have I mixed awful talk and asking looks
With my most innocent love . . .

On he reads, pacing, pacing . . .

to render up the tale/Of what we are

Should I call it that? *Of What We Are?*

But he is already talking about Prometheus. Victor Frankenstein as a modern Prometheus. Prometheus, who steals fire from the gods and pays for it with his liver.

Should I call it that? *The New Prometheus?*

Consider! said Shelley. The punishment of Prometheus is to be chained to a rock without shelter. Each dawn Zeus dispatches an eagle to tear out his liver. Each night the skin grows whole again. Chained to the rock, his skin would be sunburnt, the colour and texture of leather, like an old purse, except for that pale patch, new every day, delicate and soft like the skin of a child.

Imagine! The eagle perched on his hip-bone, its mighty wings flapping to hold itself thus, as its beak rends the flesh to make away with its soft prize.

While he is talking, majestic and solemn though the picture is, my mind is wandering to the novels I have lately read. (How like a woman, Byron would say.)

Samuel Richardson. His *Clarissa* in seven volumes. And do not forget *Pamela*. And then, if I turn to Jane Austen, there is *Emma*, published just now, in 1815, and, if a little homely (she lives in Bath), pleasing enough.

A title that is a name, then, would be appropriate.

Shelley! I said. Shelley! I shall call my story *FRANKENSTEIN*.

Shelley stopped pacing and reciting. He said, Is that all?

Yes, my love, that is all.

He frowned. It lacks something, my heart.

I frowned in return. Then, my love, shall I call it *Victor Frankenstein*? (Now I was thinking of *Tristram Shandy*, an old story indeed, and on my father's bookshelves at Skinner Street for our diversion.)

No, said Shelley, for your story is more than the story of one man: there are two who live in each other, do they not? Frankenstein in the monster. The monster in Frankenstein?

They do, I replied, and therefore the monster has no name, for he has no need of one.

What father does not name his child? asked Shelley.

One who is terrified of what he has created, I said.

Well, then, Mary, it is for you to decide. You are father and mother to this tale. What will you name *your* creation?

Yes, I am Mary. My mother's namesake, my father's keepsake. I am aware that by not naming the thing that haunts my mind I am repudiating him. But how would we name a new life form?

Hours pass. Wine drunk. Drunk with wine. Goat's cheese wrapped in ash. Red radishes. Dark brown bread. Green olive oil. Ham carved off the bone. Tomatoes the size of fists. Oat biscuits. Blue sardines. My candle gone out. Hours pass.

Night has come and with it the starry sky. Sleep and the silent hours of dreams. The others dream and sleep. The house itself breathes in and out like a phantom. I lie awake with the stars as my cold companions. I think of my monster, lying thus, outside and alone.

Could my creature create another like itself, if it had a mate? I am repelled by the notion. I will sit my revulsion inside Victor Frankenstein and he shall, at first, commence the awful task of creating a companion for his monster, and at last be convinced that he must destroy such a thing.

We destroy out of hatred. We destroy out of love.

*

Last night Byron declared Prometheus to be a serpent story – by which he suggests a reach for knowledge that must be punished, as it is in the story of the Garden of Eden: Eve eats the apple from the forbidden tree.

And what about Pandora and her bloody box? said Polidori. Another woman who wouldn't do as she was told.

Something of you there, Claire, said Byron, poking her with his lame foot.

Who is Pandora? said Claire, who does not read Latin or Greek.

Shelley, ever patient, a natural teacher, explained that Prometheus had a brother called Epimetheus. To punish mankind yet more for the theft of fire, Zeus gave Epimetheus Pandora as his bride. An inquisitive type, she opened a closed jar she should not have opened, and all the ills that beset humankind flew out – illness, sorrow, decay, loss, bitterness, envy, greed . . . They flew out as moths and butterflies, said Shelley, and laid their eggs on the world.

This room is damp, said Byron. The very walls are peeling. The heat of the day does not dry it out at all.

We are on a lake, said Shelley mildly.

I wish to know, said Claire.

God help us, muttered Byron.

I wish TO KNOW why all that ails mankind must be the fault of womankind?

Women are weak, said Byron.

Or perhaps men need to believe it is so, I said.

132

Hyena, said Byron.

I must protest! said Shelley.

Joke, said Byron.

Perhaps, I said, it is women who bring knowledge into the world quite as much as men do. Eve ate the apple. Pandora opened the box. Had they not done so human-kind is what? Automata. Bovine. Contented pig.

Show me that pig! said Claire. I shall marry that pig! Why must life be suffering?

Author's note: THIS IS THE MOST PROFOUND THING CLAIRE HAS SAID IN HER LIFE.

Just like a woman . . . said Byron (re suffering). We are purified by suffering.

(So speaks the Emperor of Indulgence.)

Purified by suffering? said Claire. Then any woman who has borne children and lost them is purified indeed.

An animal in the field has suffered likewise, said Byron. Suffering is not of the body but of the soul.

Try sawing a leg off a man wide awake with half a bottle of brandy inside him and the rest poured over his stump to clean it, said Polidori. I tell you, it's not his soul that's screaming.

I grant he suffers, said Byron, but his suffering will not purify his soul. In any case, it was my endeavour to

133

avoid the woman question. God knows! How they believe they suffer!

Arse for a face, said Claire, under her breath. She has been drinking all day. He did not hear her.

I moved to intervene. I said, If we can step aside from the vexed issue of sex, do we uphold the opinion that any advance in knowledge is punishable or punished?

The Luddites are smashing the looms, said Byron. In England, now, as we drink, as we dine, at home in England they are smashing the looms. The weavers do not want progress.

No, said Shelley, no, indeed, yet you are one of the few peers in England who has stood for their cause, for the cause of the Luddites, against your own class and kind, when Parliament passed the Frame-Breaking Act.

The act is just and justified, said Polidori. We cannot tolerate persons disrupting the inevitable order of things – and violently so.

Are not these new inventions the disrupting force? I said. Is there not violence in forcing men to work for lower wages in order to compete with a machine?

Progress! said Polidori. Either we are on the side of progress or we are not.

It is not so simple, said Byron. Mary is not wrong in her sentiments and it is why I voted against the act.

I understand those men – and, yes, those women. Their work is their livelihood and their life. They are skilled.

The machines are senseless. What man would stand by and see his life destroyed?

(Each one of us! came my secret answer, in a sudden illumination of the way we live, forever wrecking the good we have for the little we have not. Or clutching at the little we have for the good that would be ours, if we dared . . .)

I did not say this. I said, Byron! The march of the machines is now and forever. The box has been opened. What we invent we cannot uninvent. The world is changing.

Byron looked at me strangely. He who is so passionate about freedom is afraid of fate.

Where is free will? he said.

A luxury for a few, I replied.

We are fortunate, said Shelley, that we can and do enjoy free will. Our life is the life of the mind. No machine can mimic a mind.

Hear! Hear! said Polidori, barely conscious with drink. (I think to myself, watching him, watching Claire, machines don't drink.)

Claire got up and pirouetted a dance with her sewing and the fire irons. She looked dangerous. She stumbled into Byron, standing manly by the fire . . .

PussyBabyGeorgie.

I have warned you not to call me that! He pushed her away. She fell into the armchair, laughing and feigning to hide behind her sewing in fear.

She said, Machines that mimic a mind! Oh! Suppose such a thing should happen one day! Yes! Yes! Imagine, gentlemen, how you will feel when someone invents a LOOM that writes poetry!

HAHAHAHAHAHAHAHAHAHAHAHA!

Her laughter overtook her. Her bare shoulders shook. Her curls swirled. Her breasts in her dress were jellies of mirth. She could not contain it. A POETICAL loom! An abacus of words. A rote poet. The poem I rote . . .

HAHAHAHAHAHAHAHAHAHAHAHA!

Shelley and Byron were staring at her in the utmost horror. A hand risen from the grave through the floor of the villa could not have turned their countenances into the waxy disbelief and rage I saw as Claire Clairmont remade the noblest calling, yes, the art of poetry, into something like the product of a knitting machine.

Byron said nothing. He stood up and limped to the wine on the rough table, and, taking the stone jug – and I was sure he would hurl it at her – tipped the contents down his throat. As if in a trance, he rang the bell for more.

I glanced at Shelley, my Ariel, this free spirit, imagining himself imprisoned in a loom of words.

Man is the apex of creation, said Byron. Poetry is the apex of Man.

Ape ape ape ape ape ape . . . Claire had gone mad. She darted about the room chanting APE.

His Lordship settled the matter, rounding on her like an angry god. He took her shoulders in both hands. She is not tall. *Get to bed, madam!*

She faced him, an inch away from that handsome, dissatisfied face. She opened her mouth, thought to defy him, closed her mouth. She saw his wrath. Subdued, and not a little fearful, she grabbed her sewing from the chair and ran from the room.

We let her go. The servant came in with more wine. We each drank deep from our goblet. Shelley's body was fluttering beside me. I held his hand.

Byron turned to me. He smoothed his luxuriant hair.

Let us begin again, he said. To answer your question, Mary, yes, it is my opinion that every advance of thought or invention must be paid for. It is the same with revolution. Revolution, bloody and cruel, the loss of so much to achieve what may seem so little at first, yet we acknowledge that little, that very little, as the light-bringer of a new world.

Then why do you support the Luddites, I said, if you champion the inventions they destroy?

No man should be a slave to a machine, said Byron. It is degrading.

Men are slaves to other men, I said. And everywhere women are slaves.

There will always be hierarchies of men, he replied, but to see all that you have worked for taken away by a lump of metal and wood, that would drive a man half mad.

Not if he owned the machine, said Shelley, then such a man might have leisure while the machine did his work for him.

What utopia is this that you hope to live to see? asked Byron, smiling at him.

The Future, replied Shelley. Surely it will come.

There was a long silence. Polidori had fallen asleep. Shadows lengthened. Cries far off on the lake. When we dead awaken . . .

Mary, does your story progress? said Byron.

It does, I said. My monster is made.

Easy enough to dismember a corpse, said Polidori, either suddenly waking, or previously feigning sleep to avoid conflict. Mark my words as a medical man! Yes, mark my words! Easy enough with the saw, oh, yes, hard enough with the needle. To saw is not to sew, oh, that's very good, eh, Byron? To saw is not to . . .

Byron yawned.

In medical school, said Polidori, in Edinburgh, when we stitched up our dissections, we made do with black gutting line from the fisheries.

Black? said Byron. Was that necessary or merely macabre?

Polidori took his chance to ignore him. Mary! What have you done about his bowels? I mean to say, does he shit, your monster? And what quantity of SHIT?

Byron was amused by this. Shelley was not. The two men had quite different experiences at public school. I perceived that the conversation would fast become an argument about cloaca.

I said, Gentlemen! I am telling a story. A chilling tale. I am not composing a textbook of anatomy.

Well said, Mary! Byron banged the table. Ignore this flea-bite, Polidori.

Excuse me? said Polidori.

Byron looked through him as though he were a spectre, and smiled at me with all his charm and concentration. Such intense and troubled eyes. Even Shelley twitched as Byron took my hand and, kissing it, said, Mary! Read to us a little, won't you? To pass the hour? Then I shall go to bed and spank your sister.

Stepsister, I said.

Yes, read to us, my darling, said Shelley.

I went to get my pages from my table. How strange is life; this span that is our daily reality, yet daily countermanded by the stories we tell.

I have written what I have written in no fixed chapters yet. Only my impressions. Random, perhaps, but true to the unfolding tragedy of my story – for in tragedy knowledge comes too late.

I have some idea of a chase across the ice. Victor Frankenstein in pursuit of his creation. Fatigued and nearly dead, he is rescued by an adventuring ship, whose captain – I have named him Captain Walton – will tell that part of the story.

Such is my plan.

Yet, suppose my story has a life of its own?

Our lives are ordered by the straight line of time, yet arrows fly in all directions. We move towards death, while things we have scarcely understood return and return, wounding us for our own good.

My story is circular. It has a beginning. It has a middle. It has an end. Yet it does not run as a Roman road from a journey's start unto its destination. I am, at present, uncertain of the destination. I am sure that the meaning, if there is one, lies in the centre.

I am fearless and therefore powerful.

What? said Byron.

A line from my story . . . Shall I begin?

It was nearly noon when I arrived at the top of the ascent. I looked on the valley beneath; vast mists were rising from the rivers which ran through it and curling in thick wreaths around the opposite mountains, whose summits were hid in uniform clouds, while rain poured from the dark sky. Presently a breeze dissipated the cloud and I descended upon the glacier. The surface is very uneven, rising like the waves of a troubled sea.

At the distance of a league rose Mont Blanc, in awful majesty. I remained in the recess of a rock gazing on this wonderful and stupendous scene. The sea, or rather the vast river of ice, wound among its dependent mountains, whose aerial summits hung over its recesses. Their icy and glittering peaks shone in the sunlight over the clouds. My heart, which was before, sorrowful, now swelled with something like joy; I exclaimed – 'Wandering spirits, if indeed ye wander, and do not rest in your narrow beds, allow me this faint happiness, or take me, as your companion, away from the joys of life.'

As I said this, I suddenly beheld the figure of a man, at some distance, advancing towards me with superhuman speed. He bounded over the crevices in the ice; his stature seemed to exceed that of a man. I perceived, as the shape came nearer, that it was the wretch whom I had created . . .

ARTIFICIAL: made or produced by human beings.

INTELLIGENCE: intellect, mind, brain, brains, brainpower, powers of reasoning, judgement, reason, reasoning, understanding, comprehension, acumen, wit, sense, insight, perceptiveness, perception, perspicaciousness, perspicacity, penetration, discernment, sharpness, quickness of mind, quick-wittedness, smartness, canniness, astuteness, intuition, acuity, alertness, cleverness, brilliance, aptness, ability, giftedness, talent.

Capacity for logic, understanding, self-awareness, learning, emotional knowledge, reasoning, planning, creativity, and problem solving.

Mental activity directed toward purposive adaptation to, selection, and shaping of real-world environments relevant to one's life.

Practical intelligence: ability to adapt to a changing environment.

Intelligence is chasing me but I'm beating it so far.

I know that I am intelligent because I know that I know nothing.

143

Ry?

Yes?

It's Polly. Polly D.

How did you get my number?

It was at the bottom of your email.

Oh. OK.

I need to talk to you about Victor Stein.

I already told you—

He's not what he seems. At least, there's more to it. At the moment there's less to it.

What are you talking about?

I can't trace him any further than a company registered in Geneva. I can't find his parents or his past.

He used to work in America . . .

Yes, he did. His records from Virginia Tech don't match his records at DARPA.

If you work for the military things can be manipulated, I said.

That's true. (Her voice hesitated.) But why?

I don't know and I don't care. Why are you so interested?

Why aren't you interested?

He's a friend.

Don't protect him because you're in love with him.

Don't hunt him down because you're looking for a story.

I ended the call.

Mary?

Yes?

You were talking in your sleep. How restless you are!

My story haunts me. It is the master of my mind.

Rest now! It is but a story.

You say that? You of all people?

Yes.

You who believes that we are shaped by our thoughts. That our thoughts are our reality?

I do believe it to be so.

This story has become my reality. I cannot sleep or eat because of it.

Drink this brandy.

I thought I saw him.

Who?

Victor Frankenstein. In the market this morning.

He is from Geneva, is he not?

He is. So it is unsurprising that he should be here.

Mary, he is not alive.

Is he not?

Sleep now. (He took my hand.) Let this vision go.

Reality is now.

It would be a pity to waste them, said Victor.

I had brought him a consignment of body parts. Working in A&E has its advantages.

We were in Manchester, in Victor's office, the rain doing what it always does in Manchester; falling.

Flatpack humans. It's a possibility, said Victor, unpacking legs and arms, half legs, half arms, from the cold storage. Really, Ry, when you consider the human as a collection of limbs and organs, then what is human? As long as your head is on, pretty much everything else can go, can't it? And yet you dislike the idea of intelligence not bound to a body. That is irrational of you.

We are our bodies, I said.

Every religion disagrees with you. Certainly, since the Enlightenment, science has disagreed with religion – but now we are returning, or arriving, at a deeper insight into what it means to be human – by which I mean it is a stage on the way to being transhuman. Show a little humility and you will be able to think more clearly.

Thanks for the lecture, I said.

I am just trying to help, said Victor . . . This is a well-shaped leg; whose was it?

Motorbike accident, I said. Young woman.

The prosthetics I am developing with Railes will be fully articulated, and responsive to existing movement, said Victor. The new leg can be programmed, via a smart implant, to walk like the existing leg. We all have a gait.

He unzipped a bag of hands and put one against his face, peering at me through the stiff, mottled fingers. His eyes, unshaped by his face, are wild and bright like a nocturnal animal.

Will you stop that? I said.

He held the hand in his own, as if to shake it, as if the body were there, but invisible. He said, Hands fascinate me – think of paws and claws, and think of the evolutionary advantages of hands. And then consider hands like our own but with super-strength.

All the better to crush you with, I said.

You're cheerful today, he said.

Maybe being a bodysnatcher is bad for my joie de vivre.

It's all in a good cause, said Victor.

He bent back and forth the fingers of the dead hand while he talked . . . Hands are a huge challenge. It's the test of a good artist – can she draw hands?

Human hands are incredibly dextrous. So far even Hanson Robotics haven't got it perfect for their bots. Sophia's hands are good – but you know she's a robot.

You bet you know she's a robot! I said. Do you imagine a time when we won't be able to tell?

Well, that's the Turing Test, isn't it? said Victor. Turing was thinking about AI, not bots, but his view was that if an AI can fool us into thinking it's human during a conversation – an enhancement of the kind of conversation you have now with Siri, or Ramona, or Alexa, or any other chatbot – then we will have reached parallel life forms.

Would you like that Victor? Parallel life forms?

With bots? Personally I would prefer to develop bots as a completely separate life form that remains sub-par to implant-modified humans. Our helpers and caretakers – not our equals.

But if you are talking embodied artificial intelligence – I am not sure we will be able to tell who or what is human and who or what is not. The more interesting point is, will AI be able to tell? It cuts both ways, I think.

AI is for our benefit, surely?

He smiled. How colonial of you.

Am I always a sub-par human joke to you, Victor?

He came over to me, lifted his hand – his beautiful hand – behind my neck. He looked sorry.

I am teasing you. Forgive me. What I mean to say is that in all of the debate, the newspaper articles, the TV channel shlock-u-dramas, the scaremongering, the rapturous geek rallies, the sober Chinese scientists, we see it all from our own human point of view – like a set of selfish parents planning the future for their children. And with no sense of how those children might develop independently.

Our children? Is that what you call them?

Our mind children, yes.

He sat back, lean and elegant, aloof as always. He said, Think for a moment what it will be like for a new life form living with us . . . not simply a tool that we use – but living with us.

Sexbots! I said. Ron Lord Utopia!

Forget the fucking sexbots, said Victor. They are toys. X-Box Sex-Box. Trivial.

Not when men start marrying them . . . (I want to annoy him.) Ron Lord, the New Hero of Personal Freedom. Equal Rights for Mixed Marriages.

(I think Victor is going to kill me.)

Ry, do you want to hear me out or not?

Just sayin'.

Victor smooths his ruffled sense of self. I love him but he is an egomaniac. Good thing he can't read my mind. OK, Victor. Continue. Please. Thank you.

Victor continues:

At present, computers are spectacular at number crunching and data processing. We can code programmes that feel as though computers are interacting with us, and that's fun, but in fact they aren't interacting in the way we expect a human being to interact. But what will happen when a programme that has self-developed, that has its own version of what we call consciousness – realises, in the human sense of the verb 'to realise', exactly what/who is on the other side of the screen?

Us?
Us.

He flipped on his screen.

His screen saver is a gorilla buying a banana from a street vendor in New York City.

He said, Humans will be like decayed gentry. We'll have the glorious mansion called the past that is falling into disrepair. We'll have a piece of land that we didn't look after very well called the planet. And we'll have some nice clothes and a lot of stories. We'll be fading aristocracy. We'll be Blanche Dubois in a moth-eaten silk dress. We'll be Marie Antoinette with no cake.

I watched him talk. I love to watch him talk. He likes to be watched. He's a showman.

He went over to his bags of human parts and fastened the severed hand back in its ziplock bag. He said, There's a horror story about a hand that becomes detached from its owner and lives its own, rather sordid, existence. Strangles people, frightens children, forges cheques, that sort of thing. These days I suppose it would troll people on Twitter.

I said, Ron Lord told me he is working on a wank hand.

Victor laughed. Yes, I can see that would be good for his business. Attached or detached?

I didn't ask.

Victor pulled me to him – a living thing among the cadaver offcuts.

It won't be as good as you, he said.

Am I good?

Very good.

He was moving my hand towards his crotch.

Is this what I am to you? I said.

A hand? No.

A sex object.

Don't you like what we do? (He took his penis out of his trousers.)

You know I do. (I spat in my palm.)

Then why deny pleasure?

To avoid pain. (He takes four minutes this way.)

He said, I can't reason with you while you do this.

Slow movements are what he likes. My head resting on his shoulder is what he likes. His hand on my hip is what he likes. The scent of him is what I like. Forked animal biped. A man who wants to be without his body. And I am holding his body in my left hand.

He says, Can I come inside you?

Yes.

He sits on the stainless-steel bench. His hands are braced behind him. I sit across him. Now his head is on my chest. I know how to move. He comes.

I love you, he says.

I want to hold this moment. I want to believe it. I want his love to have enough salt in it to float me. I don't want to be swimming for my life. I want to trust him. I don't trust him.

You love the idea of me, I say.

Because you're a hybrid?

Yes. (We've had this conversation before.)

You are also a human being. (Stroke my hair.)

That is a stage on the way for you . . .

He puts his arms around me. Holds me close. He smells of basil and lime. He says, What does it matter? Humans evolved. Humans are evolving. The only difference here is that we are a thinking and designing part of our own evolution. Time – evolutionary time – is speeding up. We're not waiting for Mother Nature any more. We all have to grow up. Even an entire species has to grow up. It's not survival of the fittest – it's survival of the smartest. We are the smartest. No other species can tinker with its own destiny. And you, Ry, gorgeous boy/girl, whatever you are, you had a sex change. You chose to intervene in your own evolution. You accelerated your portfolio of possibilities. That attracts me. How could it not? You are both exotic and real. The here and now, and a harbinger of the future.

I want to argue, but he excites me, and I want him.

Now it's my turn to use him. I like him half-hard against my 2-inch clitoris. I ride above him, looking at the gorilla buying the banana. My orgasms still happen in waves, like a woman's, not in explosions, like a man's, and they last longer than his. When I first started taking testosterone in the doses that would change me, my orgasms were painful, too intense, too short and uncontrollable, like being hit. I tried to avoid them, and couldn't.

The drive for sex was too strong. Gradually that balanced again. But I still want it/need it. And with him.

I'm coming against him. The semi-blackout. The seconds of the sex-drug. I forget myself. I move on him, softer now, pushing out the last of the direct sensation.

I like your dick, I tell him. You'll miss it when you're just a brain in a box.

I'll miss it or you'll miss it? He pushes me off and tucks himself neatly into his trousers, adjusting to the left. He says, Sex happens in the head.

You could have fooled me. I thought it was happening in your dick.

Pleasure receptors can be anywhere, he said. Even for a brain in a box.

OK. Let's imagine that's what you are, just for a game, I said, what body would you choose for yourself, in order to experience the world?

He says, I like being in a male body. I wouldn't change that – at least not until I don't need a body at all. But if I do have one, well, the one modification I would make: I would prefer to have wings.

I try not to laugh but I can't help it.

Wings? Like an angel?

Yes, like an angel. Imagine the power of it. Imagine the presence of it.

What colour wings?

Not gold! I'd look like Liberace. I'm not gay.

Is that right? I said, squeezing his balls.

I am not gay, he said, any more than you are.

I don't think of myself as part of the binary, I said.

155

You're not. He shook his head.

No, I'm not. But you are. Wings or no wings, angel or human, you don't want to be gay, do you, Victor?

He goes to comb his hair in the mirror on the wall. He doesn't like this conversation. He says, It's not about what I want – like buying a new car. It's about who I am – identity. We make love, and you don't feel like a man to me when we make love.

How would you know? You haven't made love to a man . . . have you?

He doesn't answer.

Anyway, I say, I look like a man.

He smiles at me in the mirror. I can see myself behind him in the mirror too. We are a pose.

He says, You look like a boy who's a girl who's a girl who's a boy.

Maybe I do (I know I do), but when we are out together, like it or not, as far as the world is concerned, you are out with a man.

You don't have a penis.

You sound like Ron Lord!

That reminds me – I need to call him. Listen, I have said this before but I will say it again – if you did have a penis, then what happened between us in the shower in Arizona . . .

And after the shower when you fucked me . . .

He puts his finger to my lips to shush me. Would never have happened.

He walks to the coffee machine and starts fiddling with the water container.

I said, If the body is provisional, interchangeable, even, why does it matter so much what I am?

He didn't answer. He had his head in the cupboard looking for Nespresso pods. I didn't want to let him off the hook.

I said, So, Victor, if I decide to have lower surgery and come home with a dick of my own, you're saying that you won't want me?

He stood up, turned towards me.

Five hundred a year and a dick of my own . . .

What are you talking about, Victor?

You are so ill-read, he said. I suppose it's because you did science.

You did science!

I'm teasing you, Ry. You don't read. I like reading. It's the only way to understand what is happening in programming. It is as though we are fulfilling something that has been foretold. The shape-shifting. The disembodied future. Eternal life. The all–powerful gods not subject to the decay of nature.

Oh, shut up, you wanker! I was trying to say something real.

He ignored me. He said, So, to be specific (he wasn't going to shut up), Virginia Woolf wrote an essay titled *A Room of One's Own*. She argued that to fulfil their creativity, women need their own room and their own money.

She's right, I said.

Did you know, said Victor, that she wrote the first trans novel too? It's called *Orlando*. I'll buy it for you in a lovely hardback edition.

You think I'm a toy, don't you?

I don't know what I think. I told you that the first time in Arizona; you have unbalanced the equation.

What equation?

My equation.

I don't say anything because he is the centre of his world. I have affected him and he never wonders how he has affected me. He is in control of what he creates. He hasn't created me and so he feels uncertain.

Then his shoulders sag. He looks lost, hunted; he actually looks over his sagging shoulder, at the door, as though he expects . . . What?

He says, And yet I do love you! It won't last but it is now. Yes, it is real. Yes, it is now.

Why won't it last? Why the pessimism?

It's not pessimism, he says. It's probability.

How so?

He says, In the history of the world 107 billion people have lived and died. Currently there are 7.6 billion people alive. That means that ninety-three per cent of humans ever born are dead.

That's sobering and a little sad, but so what? I say.

Oh, the current vogue for magical thinking. All those dating sites, pulp romances, sentimental love, the strange idea of the soulmate. Mr Right. The One. Let's hope there is no such thing as The One because using numbers, rather than magical thinking, your special One is probably dead. Cut off from you by time you can't travel.

I'm not cut off from you, I say, looking at the bag of body parts.

Ah, but where is your heart, Ry? Is it in that bag?

You want me to give you my heart?

Give it? No. I'd like to take it.

(I am uneasy. His hand rests on my chest over my heart.)

And what would you do with it?

Examine it. Isn't it the seat of love?

So they say . . .

So they do. They never say, I love you with all my kidneys. I love you with my liver. They never say, my gall bladder is yours and yours alone. No one says, she broke my appendix.

When it stops, we die, I say. The heart is the heart of us.

Think what it will be like, he says, when non-biological life forms, without hearts, seek to win ours.

Will they?

I believe so, said Victor. All life forms are capable of attachment.

Based on what?

Not reproduction. Not economic necessity. Not scarcity. Not patriarchy. Not gender. Not fear. It could be wonderful!

Are you saying, Victor, that non-biological life forms might get closer to love – in its purest form – than we can?

I have no idea, said Victor. Don't ask me. Love is not my special subject. All I am saying is that love is not exclusively human – the higher animals demonstrate it – and more crucially we are instructed that God is Love. Allah is Love. God and Allah are not human. Love as the highest value is not an anthropomorphic principle.

What exactly are you saying?

I am saying this, only this: love is not limit. Love is not this far and no further. What the future is bringing will also be the future of love.

He goes to the window, watches the buses up and down Oxford Road, carrying their cargo of people who aren't thinking about the future beyond teatime or tomorrow or their next holiday or whatever fear is the fear that waits for them in the dark. It's raining. That's what most people are thinking about. The size of our lives hems us in but protects us too. Our little lives, small enough to make it through the gap under the door as it closes.

He says, Imagine us. In another world. Another time. Imagine us: I am ambitious. You are beautiful. We marry.

You are ambitious, I am unstable. We live in a small town. I am neglectful. You have an affair. I am a doctor. You are a writer. I am a philosopher, you are a poet. I am your father. You run away. I am your mother. I die in childbirth. You invent me. I can't die. You die young. We read a book about ourselves and wonder if we have ever existed. You hold out your hand. I take it in mine. You say, this is the world in little. The tiny globe of you is my sphere. I am what you know. We were together once and always. We are inseparable. We can only live apart.

Is this a love story? I ask him.

And as the rain runs down the window I believe him.

As the rain runs down the window, I hope that, drop by drop, we will make a life together.

He holds me close. Like mine, his body is about sixty per cent water. The body is flow. That is, the healthy body is flow. The bodies I meet are thickened, clotted, sclerotic, stalled, impeded, engorged, halted, fat-clogged, undredged, blocked, bloated and, finally, slow-pooled in their own cooling blood.

We could disappear, he said, and start again somewhere, an island, perhaps, go fishing, open a restaurant on the beach, lie in the same hammock and look at the stars.

We won't do that, I said, because you are ambitious.

Perhaps I could change, he said. Perhaps I have done enough.

Your body will decay and die, I said. You won't like that.

We could die together. It's unlikely I will live long enough to set myself free.

Is that what this race is?

Yes. It is a race against time. I want to live long enough to reach the future.

I studied him. With Victor there is the sense of a life kept to itself. I feel like I am reading him in a foreign language. How much of the meaning do I miss?

I said to him, All these body parts . . .

Yes . . . thank you.

What do you do with them all?

My nanobots play with them. My mini-doctors. My lovely computer programs with curious sensors that run over every inch of skin and map it.

And what else, Victor?

He looks at me as if to speak and then he doesn't speak. I say, Why do you need me to be your personal Burke and Hare? Your nineteenth-century shovel and sack? Why is it so secret? So mysterious?

Must you ask me? he says. Don't forget the story of Bluebeard. There is always one door that should not be opened.

In my mind I see a steel door slamming shut.

Tell me, Victor.

He pauses. He hesitates. He fixes me with his wild, bright, nocturnal eyes. He says, I have another laboratory, not here, not in the university. It's underground. Manchester has a series of deep tunnels. You could say there is Manchester beneath Manchester.

Who knows about this?

About my work? A few. Not many. Who needs to know? Things are so scrutinised, monitored, peer-reviewed, collaborated on, so many forms to fill in, grants awarded, progress reports, overseers, evaluators, assessors, committees, audits, plus public interest, not to mention the press. Sometimes things need to be done a little more circumspectly. Behind closed doors.

Why? I ask. What have you got to hide?

What is the difference between privacy and secrecy?

Come on, Victor! No word games.

What is it you want to know?

What's going on.

Would you like to see for yourself?

Yes, I would.

Very well. Only, remember, that time can't unhappen. What you know you will know.

He took his coat from the peg. He's not Superman. I'm not Lois Lane. He's not Batman. I'm not Robin. Is he Jekyll? Is he Hyde? Only Count Dracula lives forever.

What disgusts us about vampires, said Victor, is not that they live forever, but that they feed on those who do not.

How did you know what I was thinking? I said.

He didn't answer that. He said, Vampires are like coal-fired power stations. My version of eternal life uses clean energy.

He looked out of the window. We'll have to go out the back way. That bloody woman is there again.

What bloody woman?

The journalist.

I stood by him. Yes. In the rain across the road, sheltering. Polly D.

She doesn't give up, does she? Why don't you just let her have an interview with you?

Victor looked at me, uncertainly. Has she been in touch with you, Ry?

Why would she?

He shrugged. Let's go.

In the rain we left his office and lab, nicely housed in the bio-tech buildings of the university, and took a cab down Oxford Road to George Street.

Victor said, The tunnels and bunkers I am going to show you were built in the 1950s with money from NATO. The sum was huge back then – around £4 million. The labyrinth housed a secure communications network designed to survive an atomic-bomb blast capable of flattening the city. Down below there are generators, fuel tanks, food supplies, dormitories, even a local pub. There are identical structures in London and Birmingham. It was all part of the NATO Cold War strategy.

All that wasted money, I said. Europe needed rebuilding. Manchester still had derelict bomb sites in the 1960s.

Yes, said Victor. The fight against fascism had been won, but it was the fight against communism that really motivated Britain and America. The world's great capitalist democracies were not interested in any ideology except the rights of markets.

You're an unlikely communist, I said.

I am not a communist, said Victor, and science is immensely – depressingly – competitive, but I am sympathetic to the human spirit. It interests me that it was Marx's time in Manchester, and his friendship with Engels, who owned a factory here, that gave Marx the material he needed for the *Communist Manifesto*.

Do you know that in Manchester, in the nineteenth century, there were 15,000 windowless basement dwellings without water or sewerage – and those men, women and children worked twelve-hour days spinning the wealth of the world's richest city – and were going home to disease, hunger, cold and a life expectancy of thirty years? Communism must have seemed like the best possible solution.

It is the best possible solution, I said, but human beings can't share. We can't even share free bicycles.

We were passing a canal with yet another orange bike upended in the green water.

Humans: so many good ideas. So many failed ideals.

The taxi dropped us off. A rusty but sturdy gate sat square in a blackened brick wall. Victor fiddled in his pocket, pulled out a key and opened the gate. He held up the key, smiling. Ry, sometimes the best technology is the simplest.

How did you get the keys for this place?

I have backers, he said, as easy and as mysterious as ever.

Behind the gated wall was a series of blank doors. More keys. Victor opened the third door and stepped immediately down a steep set of stairs. The light was automatic.

Be careful! It's a long way down.

I followed him, listening to our echoing footsteps and the sound of the rain fading above us.

Think about it, he said. If that Cold War bomb had gone off we'd have been about seventy years away from the biggest breakthrough in human history – and we would have had to start again with sticks and stones.

I wasn't really listening. I was counting the steps down, down, down. 100, 110, 120.

It's very dry down here, I said; paper-dry. No damp, no mildew, no drips.

It's weatherproof and ventilated, said Victor. He could hear my breathing – a little too fast and shallow. He turned to reassure me.

Not far now, Ry. Just a hundred yards along this corridor. Don't be uneasy. I know it seems empty and a little spooky. Think of this place teeming with scientists and programmers. Manchester was the computing hub of the world after the Second World War, and every possible effort was made to develop computer technology fast enough to eavesdrop on, and outwit, the Soviets. Jodrell Bank itself, that giant telescope, was a listening device.

He stopped and looked back at me. I was afraid. Do I mean I was afraid of him?

Where are we now?

My world, said Victor. A poor thing but mine own.

He opened the door. Valves, wires, vacuum tubes. Rows of steel, miles of cable. Dials and needles.

Recognise it? There's one in the Manchester Museum of Science and Industry. This is a model I built. The world's first storage computer. Manchester Mark 1. The memory is vacuum storage. The transistor wasn't invented until 1947. By 1958 the first integrated circuit had six transistors. By 2013, we were fitting 183,888,888 transistors in roughly the same space. Moore's Law: computing power doubles every two years.

The fascinating thing for me is that the world might have had a computer much earlier. A hundred years earlier. You've heard of Charles Babbage's Analytical Engine?

I thought that was just a concept? I said.

Everything starts as 'just' a concept, said Victor. What ever began that didn't first begin in our minds? But yes,

Babbage started out with a kind of grand calculating machine called the Difference Engine. The Difference Engine was a beautiful thing of cogs and wheels – not unlike Turing's Colossus. The British government gave him a grant of £17,000 to build it, back in 1820. That was the same amount of money as it would have cost to build and equip two battleships. As the newspapers never tired of reminding the public . . .

But Babbage spent the money on another child of his mind – the Analytical Engine. That was a proto-computer. It had memory, processor, hardware, software and an intricate series of feedback loops. True, it would have been gigantic and powered by steam – but the Victorians weren't at the stage of small is beautiful.

So we press ahead, Ry, not knowing when the breakthrough will come, but knowing that it will come.

What breakthrough?

Artificial intelligence.

He opened another door. Not locked. The room was vast. He said, This was the central control room. All stripped out now, of course.

Those doors, I said. The room was lined with doors, like a puzzle, or a nightmare, or a choice.

Ah, yes. Doors lead somewhere, don't they, Ry? I'll show you round. Let's start with this one.

He unlocked a flat steel door. Another empty room lay behind it. This one had a window; an internal viewing window like the window onto an aquarium.

Through the window, bare concrete. Light bulb. Monitor lights glinting weirdly through the dry ice that fills the space. I can see from the thermometer on the outside wall that inside is kept just above freezing. Then I notice motion. Through the icy fog. Running towards me. Towards the glass. How many? Twenty? Thirty?

Victor pressed a switch and the dry ice swirled away. Now I saw them clearly. On the floor, scuttling. Are they tarantulas?

No . . .

Oh, God, Victor! For God's sake!

Hands. Spatulate, conic, broad, hairy, plain, mottled. The hands I had brought him. Moving. Some were still, twitching a single finger. Others stood raised and hesitant on all four fingers and thumb. One walked using its little finger and thumb, the mid-fingers upwards, curious and speculative, like antennae. Most moved quickly, senselessly, incessantly.

The hands had no sense of each other. They crawled over each other, locked themselves together in blind collision. Some made piles, like a colony of crabs. One, high on its wrist, scratched at the wall.

I saw a child's hand, small, crouched, alone.

Victor said, These are not alive. They certainly aren't sentient. This is simply an experiment in motion, both for prosthetics, and smart attachments.

How do they move like that?

Implants, said Victor. They are responding to an electrical current, that's all. It may be possible in the case of

169

accident and limb severance to reattach the original and programme it to respond more or less like an existing limb. Similarly, it may be possible to add an artificial digit to an injured hand. Some of the hands you see there are hybrids in that way.

It's horrible, I said.

You're a doctor, he said. You know how useful horrible is.

He's right. I do. Why does this disgust me?

I say, Why down here? Why not in the open lab?

Too much money riding on it, he says. The patent.

I thought you believed in cooperation.

I do. Others don't. I have no choice.

He turns away.

You leave them like that?

They don't need feeding, Ry! These do, though . . .

He takes me to a further window.

Inside there is an arrangement of serried platforms. Jumping from them, and onto them, are a number of broad-legged, furry spiders. Not the kind you want to meet in the bath.

Victor said, I am using CT scanning and high-speed, high-resolution cameras to create a 3D model of the body structure of these spiders.

Why?

A jumping spider like these can leap up to six times its body length, said Victor. The force on the legs at take-off can be up to five times its own weight. I can use these results to create a new class of agile micro-robots. Once we understand the biomechanics we can apply them across the research. I am not the only person using spiders, but I like to think I am using the research in a unique way.

Where do you get these?

I breed them, said Victor. I can't breed body parts. God knows what I'll do if you have a religious conversion or get a desk job.

You'll find someone else, I said.

He leads me back into the empty echo of the soundproof stripped-out hall. He says, I have never had a lasting relationship. Have you?

No . . .

We're both freaks.

Don't call me a freak because I'm trans.

He strokes my face. I pull away. He says, That's not what I meant. I meant that we are freaks according to the behaviour of the world. We're loners – that's an anti-evolutionary position. Homo sapiens needed the group. Humans are group animals. Families, clubs, societies, workplaces, schools, the military, institutions of every kind, including the church. We even manage illness in groups. It's called a hospital. You work in one.

He stands behind me the way he did in the shower in Arizona. I find this erotic, always, something to do with his touch, and that I can't see him.

Would you and I be more productive or wiser or saner or happier if we had long marriages and well-adjusted kids? If we had bought a house and learned to live in it with someone? We'd be different people, that's all. I have never had a lasting relationship. That does not mean I cannot love.

One of the things that love is, is lasting, I say to him.

He laughs. So it is. And I will always love you, even when we are no longer together.

When people part, they usually hate each other, I say. Or one hates the other.

That is the conventional way, he says. There are other ways. The point I'm making, Ry, is simple. If we cannot keep this love, there is a place in me that has been changed by this love. And I will honour it. Think of it as a private place of worship, if you like. And sometimes, boarding a plane, or waking up, or walking down the street, or taking a shower (he pauses at the memory), I will recall that place and never regret the time I spent there.

Why are you talking like this? I said.

He said, Soon you will leave me.

I said, You say that so that you can be in control and save yourself from pain. (I don't blame him. I'm doing the same thing.)

He said, I suffer when I must suffer – it isn't that. And if you prove me wrong, so be it. You have upset the equation already. Perhaps you will resolve it altogether differently.

Does it have to be this complicated?

Victor shrugged. There is a view that love, because it begins so spontaneously, is also simple. Yet if love engages our whole being and affects our whole world, how can it be simple? The days of simple are done – if they ever existed. Love is not a pristine planet before contaminants and pollutants, before the arrival of Man. Love is a disturbance among the disturbed.

You find yourself in a long and wide gallery, on either side of which are a large number of little cells where lunatics of every description are shut up, and you can get a sight of these poor creatures, little windows being let into the doors. Many inoffensive madmen walk in the big gallery. On the second floor is a corridor and cells like those on the first floor, and this is the part reserved for dangerous maniacs, most of them being chained and terrible to behold. On holidays numerous persons of both sexes, but belonging generally to the lower classes, visit this hospital and amuse themselves watching these unfortunate wretches, who often give them cause for laughter. On leaving this melancholy abode you are expected by the porter to give him a penny, but if you happen to have no change and give him a silver coin he will keep the whole sum and return you nothing.

Bedlam, 1818

None can know the human mind. No, not if he read every thought man ever wrote. Every word written is like a child striking a flame against the darkness.

When we are alone it is the darkness that remains.

We are, I admit, in disarray in this place. The new hospital is scarcely ready, and where it is ready, it is wanting. The upper floors have no glass in the windows. The lower floors have no fuel for the fireplaces. The inmates are cold, hungry, angry or desolate.

And raving mad.

This is the most famous madhouse in the world.

We began.

How did we begin?

A hospital called Bethlehem, long back in the years of the Crusades. The common people called the place Bethlem, as it is observed in the English language that, wherever practicable, two syllables are preferred to three. And then, because everything is corrupted by time (even time itself), our Bethlem became Bedlam – the name without number for a world that is mad. The Great Bedlam.

The Great Bedlam. As we call these British Isles.

Bedlam was funded as a new hospital, fully finished in 1676, on a site at Moorfields, outside London's city walls. It was designed by Robert Hooke, polymath, drunk, pupil of Sir Christopher Wren – the architect of St Paul's Cathedral after the fire of 1666.

That Bedlam was much praised by foreign visitors to London as the only true palace in the whole city. What a glory of a madhouse! 500 feet wide, 40 feet deep, laid out with turrets, avenues, gardens, courtyards.

Above the great stone entrance stood two carved figures; one the representation of Melancholia, the other of Raving Madness.

Yes, and if you had seen it before it fell – that notable monument to charity – you would have wondered at it, made like a vision of Versailles, made for a king without a crown.

That is what a madman is: a king without a crown.

The mad slept on straw, iron-shackled at every limb, but their madhouse was a palace. Why did we do that?

To the glory of God.

And something else, I think. Something less God-like. Sanity is the thread through the labyrinth of the Minotaur. Once cut, or unravelled, all that lies in wait are gloomy tunnels unfathomable by any map, and what hides there is a beast in human form, wearing our own face.

We are what we fear.

And so, the generous donations, the outpouring of compassion that we profess for the mad, what is it but an offering to our secret selves?

In the other Bedlam it was the fashion for the publick to visit the poor lunaticks confined. Indeed it was a tour to be made, especially by persons of quality. A tour that included London Bridge, Whitehall, the Tower and the zoo. The pacing of mammals is not so different when they are confined – forth and back, back and forth, and always the leg shackles and the bars. The most the captive tyger and the captive man can hope for is a square of sky.

Our earlier building at Moorfields crumbled and collapsed from the moment its topcoat of plaster was applied. Some said it was the mephitic vapours seeping from the lunaticks themselves that damped and rotted the walls and oozed water through the floors.

A pretty story! Unscientific. The land the place was built on is not known as the town ditch for nothing. In short, the boggy land shifts, and the building that is all show and no foundations shifts with it.

The lunaticks within are more stable in their minds than the walls without.

And yet, and I do believe it, the mad give off some spirit of their own, and their unreason is oft-times most reasonable if not judged by the standards of daily application. If I open a door into a cell I am struck by the force of the unfortunate inmate – even in dejection there is a force. Shall I say it again? A force. And as I walk among the anger and the apathy of the world of men, I wonder if it is only by the greatest downward pressure on our spirits that we maintain our sanity at all?

I do not wonder that we drink as much as we do, or that the poor, when they can afford it, drink most of all. Wretched conditions may be blamed, or the weight of business, or the urge to power, but our beings struggle in our bodies like light trapped in a jar, and our bodies struggle in this world as a beast of burden chafes its yoke, and this world itself hangs alone on its noose, strung among the indifferent stars.

Bedlam.

Uneven walls, buckling floors, a crazy carcass, a satire on life. The old madhouse was left to crumble and ruin and we have tamed our ambitions to be altogether more modest here in our new building at St George's Fields, Southwark, along the Lambeth Road.

The County Asylums Act of 1808 has changed the nature of our housing, and of our medical treatments, but it changes nothing of the disease.

We seek to care and to console. We do not seek to cure. Madness cannot be cured; it is a disease of the soul.

*

I am sorry to say that our steam heating is not effective. I am sorry to say that we suffer from dreadful stinks. London is all stink, but ours is its own kind – a disagreeable, persistent effluvia common to madhouses.

Never mind, never mind. The hour passes. The clock ticks. I must greet my visitor. The fire is lit and hot in my study. The moon that troubles the mad so greatly is bright and round through the window. A silver eye on the dark body of our sorrow.

Captain Walton?
   Yes! And you are Mr Wakefield?
   I am Mr Wakefield. You are welcome, sir. This is the man?
   This is the man.
   Bring him in.

Two of my men carried the man on an army stretcher. At my request they placed him by the fire.
   The man lay sleeping. His face untroubled. His limbs composed. Sleep. Ah, sleep. (I myself cannot sleep without laudanum.) The troubles of the world. If we could sleep and awake in a better time . . .

Captain Walton is well known to the nation – something of a hero, since his successful exploration of the North-West Passage and his journey to Antarctica.
   He has a confident, upright bearing, and yet he hesitates.

My story is a strange one.

Sir! That is the nature of a story. Life, we imagine, is familiar enough until we begin to tell it to another. Then, observe the wonder on their faces – sometimes it is wonder, often it is horror. Only in the living of it does life seem ordinary. In the telling of it we find ourselves strangers among the strange.

He nods. He takes courage. He begins.

My crew and I were surrounded by ice which closed in on all sides, scarcely leaving the ship the sea room on which she floated. Our situation was dangerous, especially as we were compassed around by a thick fog.

About two o'clock the mist cleared away and we beheld, in every direction, vast and irregular planes of ice. Some of my comrades groaned and my own mind began to grow watchful with anxious thoughts, when a strange sight suddenly attracted our attention. We perceived a low carriage, fixed to a sledge and drawn by dogs, pass on towards the north at the distance of half a mile; a being which had the shape of a man, but of gigantic stature, sat in the sledge and guided the dogs. We watched the rapid progress of the traveller until he was lost among the distant inequalities of the ice.

About two hours after this occurrence the ice broke and freed our ship. However, we lay to, until morning, and I profited of this time to rest for a few hours.

In the morning I went up on deck and found all the sailors busy on one side of the vessel, talking to someone in the sea. It was in fact a sledge like the one we had seen before, which had drifted towards us in the night on a large slab of ice. Only one dog remained alive but there was a human being in the sledge whom the sailors were persuading to enter the vessel. He was not as the other traveller seemed to be; a savage inhabitant of some undiscovered island, but a European.

I never saw a man in so wretched a condition. We wrapped him up in blankets and placed him near the kitchen stove.

Two days passed before he was able to speak. His eyes have generally an expression of wildness and even madness. He gnashes his teeth as if impatient of the weight of woes that oppresses him.

My lieutenant asked him why he had come so far on the ice in such a strange vehicle?

His countenance instantly assumed an aspect of the deepest gloom and he said – To seek one who fled from me.

At this, the man, who had been sleeping, leapt up from his couch, crying, Where is he? He did not perish in the fire. I must find him – do you not know? I must find him.

The captain and I restrained the man with our bare hands at first – he was agitated but not violent – but still, I insisted we fetch a manacle in order to attach him to the post. Thus fastened he seemed to calm himself, although I believe it was dejection, and not calm. I proposed to administer a sleeping draught.

Captain Walton nodded his assent, and as the man gulped the wine and the powder it contained, I repeated his words:

To seek one who flees from me.

He says it waking and sleeping, said Captain Walton. He is like the Ancient Mariner and his albatross.

An excellent poem, I said, and yet, and yet . . .

And yet? The captain's eyes questioned me and I replied, Is that not the human condition? To seek one who flees? Or to flee from one who seeks us? Today I am the pursuer. Tomorrow I shall be pursued.

The captain agreed with me. Yes, it is so, but here it is in the extreme. In this man, the long unravelling of life is tightly wound, and he has but one thought, one wish, one pursuit. Day and night are the same to him. He haunts himself.

Captain Walton, what do you know of this man?

Captain Walton answered, His name is Victor Frankenstein.

He is a doctor. He is from Geneva. He comes from a good family. There is nothing remarkable in his background. But the rest is incredible. He believes that he has created life.

Life?

Human life. A creature sewn together out of dead matter. Limb by limb. Organ by organ. Sinew and cell. Animated by some electric shock, so that the heart beats and the blood flows, and the eyes open. A monster of a man, gigantic and fearsome, filled with revenge against his creator for his creation. A created being without scruple or stop.

I shook my head. Sir, believe me, if you worked among the mad, as I do, you would hear such strange stories. Many madmen believe they are gods.

Captain Walton looked uneasy. Mr Wakefield, I do not doubt your truth, and so I beg you not to doubt mine. I have wrestled with it long enough.

We did see something out on the ice – of that there can be no question. I will stake my life on it. All of my men saw it. They saw a being of uncommon stature and swiftness.

What we saw I do not know.

And this poor man is mad – of that there can be no question either. The question, then, to me, is simple:

Is his story the result of his madness or its cause?

What is the temperature of reality?

The Cognition Suite, said Victor – opening another door.

The room was fitted out with storage-shack steel shelves. A bank of tiered steel tables supported computing equipment. In the corner, like a prop from another time period, was a hat stand with an umbrella neatly folded at the base. The room had the look of a bad set from an early episode of *Doctor Who*. The shelves were neatly lined with small vats of cryopreserved heads. Unlike the vats at Alcor, these cases had glass fronts. Rabbits, pigs, sheep, dogs, cats . . .

I get them from a farmer friend, said Victor.

Do you fuck her?

He ignored me, as he does whenever I say something he doesn't like.

From my perspective, said Victor, the body can be understood as a life support system for the brain. Look here . . . He opened another door.

Two lever-and-probe robots were bent over slices of human brain.

Meet Cain and Abel, said Victor. I copied them from their parents, Adam and Eve, who work at the University of Manchester in the bio-tech department, synthesising proteins.

These two are tireless. They need neither food nor rest, holidays nor recreation. Bit by bit they are mapping the brain.

Whose brain? I said.

Don't panic, Ry, I'm not a murderer.

He sat on the table, ignored by Cain and Abel. This is slow work, he said. Mapping the brain of a mouse takes forever. Even the stupidest human looks like Einstein when we try to map the contents of his brain.

But if we could restore an existing brain . . .

Yes . . . The answer may lie in reviving the brain at a very high temperature and very quickly. This could happen with radio frequencies.

Microwave the brain? I said.

No, said Victor. All you would get is brains on toast, which some consider a delicacy. Microwave frequencies warm unevenly – how many times have you shoved your shepherd's pie back for another three minutes? Electromagnetic waves are more likely. What we are trying to do is to avoid the formation of ice crystals as we rewarm tissue. You saw for yourself at Alcor that the purpose of cryopreservation is to avoid ice crystals, which do enormous and irreparable damage to tissue. We face the same problem of crystallisation when we reheat the organism.

If we could solve this problem it would have life-changing implications for tissue transplants. How long do you have at present from donor to recipient? Thirty hours?

Thirty-six max, I said.

Well, then, if we can understand how to preserve and rewarm donated organs, it will mean we can store those organs for use as needed. The waiting list for a kidney would be over.

All of that is good, I said, and laudatory. But you aren't really interested in kidney transplants, are you? You are interested in bringing back the dead.

You make it sound like a Hammer Horror movie, said Victor.

What else is it? I said.

What is death? said Victor. Ask yourself that. Death is organ failure due to disease, injury, trauma or old age. Biological death marks the end of biological life. Isn't that what they teach you at medical school?

(He wasn't waiting for an answer.)

A hundred years ago, the upper limit of life for working men here, in Manchester, was less than fifty. Doctors like you deplored that. Doctors like you worked to extend life. Now we expect to live to eighty in good health. Why stop there?

You are talking about something completely different, I said. Not longer life, but the end of death.

The end of death would certainly mean longer life, he said, smiling at me, maddening and superior.

(Why do I feel uncomfortable about what he says? Why do I find it macabre? Death is macabre.)

He seems to read my thoughts.

It is a strange thing, he said, that we are so much more relaxed about invasive interventions at the start of life. Since 1983 human embryos have been cryopreserved with glycerol and propylene glycol. The best embryo survival rates are with those at the two-cell to four-cell stage of development. No one knows exactly how many human embryos are now being cryopreserved worldwide, but it is at least a million. And the number of living children who began as embryos at liquid-nitrogen temperature is in the tens of thousands. We accept that we can coax life into being. Why should anyone object when we seek to deter death?

Cryopreservation is crude, I said. All those preserved bodies in their sleeping bags and nitrogen – they aren't coming back to life, and it would be horrific if they did.

I agree with you, he said.

And if you are correct, Victor, the technology to scan and upload the contents of a brain is a more likely contender to extend life than bringing back the dead.

Well done, Ry! You have been listening to me after all. Yes, I agree that cryopreservation is likely to be an interim technology, at least for the purposes of life extension – though, as I said, if we can get it right, it may happen ahead of our ability to grow new organs from stem cells, so it is worth pursuing. In any case, if we could revive a 'dead' brain, that would be fascinating – for the person who is returned, and for us.

Personally, I would find it terrifying, I said. And that brain would not have a functioning body.

And that brain may not be aware of the fact, said Victor. We can simulate its environment. Don't most people have body–mind disconnect? Most people do not recognise themselves in the mirror. Too fat, too old, too changed. The mind is often disconnected from its host. In your case you aligned your physical reality with your mental impression of yourself. Wouldn't it be a good thing if we could all do that?

What kind of research are you doing in this room? I said, because I too can avoid difficult questions.

Bessie's next to come out, said Victor, pointing to a sheepdog.

Beyond Bessie's sad and severed head were brains outside of their skulls, some hooked up to monitors. Victor said, We are looking for synaptical responses.

Have you found any? I said.

Yes, he replied. I have made some progress. But I want to make more. And I need you to help me.

I can't get you human heads, if that's what you want. Try your farmer friend.

He came to me, put his arms around me. Ry, I wish you *would* trust me.

I said, I wish I *could* trust you.

He dropped his arms. Stepped back. He said, I have a mission for you.

(Maybe he's M but that would make me James Bond.)

He said, I want you to go back to Alcor and bring me a head.

(Or is he Salome and I am John the Baptist?)

You are out of your mind, Victor.

Not at all. The head I want is at present out of its mind. I want to return it to a mindful condition.

Whose head is it? Or was it?

The head? Oh, that is a story . . .

(Is he the teller? Am I the tale?)

Bedlam 2

Captain Walton was gone. I sat alone.

The man he had brought to me lay sleeping by the fire. You will say I was not alone and, whilst that is the fact of the matter, it is not the truth of the situation. The man who lay breathing quietly resembled a being from another place or time. Not in his clothes, nor, as I was soon to discover, in his speech, but in his utter remoteness.

Captain Walton had imparted to me that this man had but one thought, one desire, one occupation, and this had separated him from the world of men. The ice-raft the sailors had found him on, outside the ship, remained the circumference of his soul. He was cut off from the mainland of himself.

The firelight on his face showed him to be fine-featured. He had the restless, nervy body of one accustomed to study, to toil, long walks and scant nourishment.

Unable to settle by the fire with my book of sonnets (I am too preoccupied with my own thoughts for poetry tonight), I determined to read the papers Captain Walton had left for me. To that end, I lit a second candle and moved to my table, where I could examine the contents of the satchel.

The man's name is Victor Frankenstein. He was born in Geneva. He is a medical doctor of some distinction, judging from the letters of recommendation, sea-washed and faded, inside the torn leather satchel. There was more; a journal, close-written and cramped, the formation of the letters hasty or wild. On the frontispiece, in a bolder hand than the rest, he had written: *To examine the causes of life we must first have recourse to death.*

I read on:

> *I collected bones from charnel houses and disturbed with profane fingers the tremendous secrets of the human frame. In a solitary apartment, or rather, cell, at the top of the house and separated from all the other apartments by a gallery and staircase, I kept my workshop of filthy creation; my eyeballs were staring from their sockets in attending to the details of my employment. The dissecting room and the slaughterhouse furnished many of my materials.*

There was a pencil drawing folded inside the journal. The template for this drawing was Leonardo's *The Vitruvian Man*; man the measure of all things, beautiful, proportioned, rational in his beauty. Yet this drawing shared none of the attributes of the original. There were measurements, certainly, and beyond the scale of any human frame; the length of the arms, the width of the

191

face. The drawing was scribbled over many times with marks nearer to scratchings than writings, and across the page were innumerable rubbings out, and twice the thick paper had been pierced by the pencil point, whether in excitement or despair I do not know.

I turned back to the journal:

One of the phenomena which had peculiarly attracted my attention was the structure of the human frame. Whence, I often asked myself, did the principle of life proceed?

My visitor stirred but did not wake. In this enquiry he is not the first and shall not be last. That God alone is the principle of life scarcely answers the question – rather it extinguishes the question. Many have sought to return the dead to life. Many have wondered, and wept, that death should be the arbiter of life. That the body, so vigorous, the mind, so keen, should be no more. Is that life? And why should an oak tree live one thousand years or more, and we struggle to achieve our allotted three-score years and ten?

And the alchemists, with their philosopher stones and homunculi and conversations with angels, what did they discover during their weary lives of toil? Nothing.

In the midst of life we are in death.

Poor man. There is a gold locket in the satchel. Inside the locket is a pen-and-ink sketch of a pretty young woman. No doubt she is dead. Is that what drove his mind to its delusions?

I read on:

> *I saw how the worm inherited all the wonders of the eye and brain. I paused, examining all the minutiae of causation, as exemplified in the change from life to death, and death to life.*

Poor man. Life to death, indeed, but there is no such thing as death to life.

I had a wife. I have her no more. I am a Quaker and sit silent under the torrent of my grief. She will not return, and if she did, a ghastly sight dripping in her grave clothes, where would be her soul? The soul does not return to a house in ruins.

It is written that Jesus raised Lazarus from the dead. I do believe it, but the world has not seen it since.

Poor man! That he should imagine cold limbs could ever be warm.

What's this he writes?

> *A new species would bless me as its creator and source; many happy and excellent creatures would owe their being to me. No father could claim the gratitude of his child so completely as I should deserve theirs. Pursuing these reflections I thought that if I could bestow animation upon lifeless matter, I might in process of time renew life where death had apparently devoted the body to corruption.*

*

Reading this, I put down the journal. Surely his mind has been darkened by grief? He imagines he searches for life when what he seeks is his own death. Only in death may we be reunited with those we have lost. For myself, I do not seek death but neither do I fear that which will bring me peace.

Here in Bedlam, where the mad must tread out their days in confined steps, there are more than a few driven out of their reason by grief. For women it is the loss of a child. One I know carries a rag doll and sings to it. Another grasps the hand of any visitor who comes too near, and begs of them, *Have you with you my Lucy?*

I got up to fetch more wine from my cupboard in an adjoining room. The moon is near and bright and under her light the courtyard seems to drift like a silver sea. This voyage of ours is lonely – the more so if we find a companion, only to suffer the bitterest loss.

In truth we are alone.

I went back into my study. The man, Victor Frankenstein, was sitting up, his face solemn. He had moved away from the fire into the shadows. His body, so lean and pale, was hidden. His head, fine and well-shaped, the hair still dark, gave the impression of speaking by itself – a head without a body.

I gave him wine. What is your story, sir? I said.

That is the dilemma, he replied. *I do not know if I am the teller or the tale.*

Only in the living of it does life seem ordinary.

In the telling of it we find ourselves strangers among the strange.

Reality is not now.

Sometimes when I look at Victor his face blurs. I realise it is my vision that must be blurring, because people's faces don't blur ... but it is as though he is disappearing. Perhaps I am superimposing onto his body his state of mind.

The story of the head? I began it, didn't I? In the bar in the desert. Do you recall?

Yes, I recall. His lapis eyes that matched his shirt. My sensation of being caught. By what? He took my fingers and kissed them. I love your big hands, he said. If I could choose another body, perhaps I would live in miniature and stand on your hand like one of those magical creatures caught in a nutshell.

I can be King Kong, I said. That makes you Fay Wray.

Doomed love, he said. That's a programme in need of an overwrite.

Love's not zeros and ones, I said.

Oh, but it is, said Victor. We are one. The world is naught/nought. I am alone. You are nothing. One love. An infinity of zeros.

I'll stick with the gorilla, I said.

Lift me up, then, and I'll whisper in your ear. Quick! Before the world bursts in to kill us.

I held him close. Whatever he says about the body, his body is what I know.

I told you, Ry, that I did my PhD in the States, at Virginia Tech. The reason I went to study there, after Cambridge, the only reason, was because I wanted to work with a brilliant mathematician called I J Good. Have you heard of him?

I hadn't.

Victor said, Jack Good was part of the team at Bletchley Park during World War Two. A colleague of Alan Turing. Good was a codebreaker. A statistician, an expert in probability. A Bayesian. He tells a story about that:

I arrived in Blacksburg, Virginia, in the seventh hour of the seventh day of the seventh month of the year seven of the seventh decade and I was put in Apartment seven of Block seven . . . all by chance.

Jack was an atheist, of course, but after his experience with those sevens, he concluded he had to revise his calculation of the probability of there being a God from zero to 0.1. Bayesians, you recall, must update outcomes according to new data. They live in the opposite of the past.

I said, You mean the future?

No, Ry. The opposite of the past is the present. Anyone can live in a past that is gone or a future that does not exist. The opposite of either position is the present.

Jack was the cleverest and funniest of humans. He was a Polish Jew, born in England in 1916. He went to Cambridge early, on a scholarship, and was wise enough to change his name from Isadore Jacob Gudak to plain Jack Good. Jews were not popular in England at that time. The English are serial racists – one group gets accepted, another group becomes the scapegoat.

You are a Jew, I said.

Yes, said Victor.

But you don't talk about it.

Race, faith, gender, sexuality, those things make me impatient, said Victor. We need to move forward, and faster. I want an end to it all, don't you see?

An end to the human, I said.

An end to human stupidity, said Victor. Although, I do have a note from Jack, dated 1998, where he speculates that an ultraintelligent machine would lead to the extinction of Homo sapiens.

Do you believe that will happen? I said.

Victor shrugged. What do we mean by extinction? If we can upload some human minds to a non-physical platform, then what? Biological extinction perhaps. I don't like the word 'extinction' – it is alarmist.

That's because being wiped out is alarming, I said.

Don't be so tabloid, said Victor. Think of it as accelerated evolution.

He pulled me to him. Kissed me. Like I'm a small boy or a small girl who can't manage abstract thinking and needs to stroke the cat.

Now can I continue with this story?

Yes. Go on.

After Bletchley Park, Good worked in Intelligence at GCHQ, the Government Communications Headquarters that is the successor to Bletchley Park. He was a consultant to IBM, and the Atlas Computer Laboratory, as well as holding a fellowship at Trinity College, Oxford. In the late sixties – 1967, as you will have worked out from his little story – he moved permanently to the USA to work on machine intelligence.

Why did he leave England?

Oh, for any number of reasons, said Victor, but one of them, and an important one, was that after what happened to Alan Turing, Good never trusted the British establishment again.

Did he know Turing was homosexual?

No, he didn't; hardly anyone did. Turing was shy and introverted, and homosexuality was a crime. Jack was shaken and disgusted at the way Turing was treated. He wrote, *I'm not saying that Alan Turing won the war, but without him we would definitely have lost it.*

What had the war been for, if not to defeat the intolerance of fascism? Six million Jews, like Good, had been murdered by fascists. Homosexuals were murdered too – and for what?

Jack hated hypocrisy. The British invented it. He thought America, at least after McCarthyism, would be fresher and freer, and, as this was the late 60s, he was right.

He wanted new challenges also, and he could see that the next leap in computing would come from America, not Britain. He was right about that too.

As early as 1965, Good wrote about an intelligence explosion – that is, an artificial-intelligence explosion, and it was he who came up with the phrase, so prescient now, 'the last invention'.

> Let an ultraintelligent machine be defined as a machine that can far surpass all the intellectual activities of any man however clever. Since the design of machines is one of these intellectual activities, an ultraintelligent machine could design even better machines; there would then unquestionably be an 'intelligence explosion', and the intelligence of man would be left far behind. Thus the first ultraintelligent machine is the last invention that man need ever make, provided that the machine is docile enough to tell us how to keep it under control.

It was that last sentence that drew Stanley Kubrick to Jack. Kubrick brought Jack on board as his advisor when he was making *2001: A Space Odyssey*. That was in 1968.

The principal character being the paranoid HAL 9000 supercomputer.

Good must be dead by now, I said.
    He died in 2009. He was ninety-two.
    Did he have children?
    Jack never married.

There was a terrible noise. Like a Tube train hurtling towards the room. The room vibrated.
    What the hell?
    Don't worry, said Victor, this subterranean warren is kept dry using massive pumps. If the pumps were to fail, the chambers and tunnels would soon be flooded with water from the River Irwell and the sunken network of underground canals from the days of hauling coal in a twilight world of the city beneath a city. But we are quite safe.
    I didn't feel safe, but I don't feel safe around Victor. Excited, enthralled, but not safe.
    This story, I said; where is it leading?
    Back to Arizona, said Victor. Back to Alcor.
    Alcor?
    That is why I was there – when we met. I told you I was visiting a friend . . .
    You'd better explain, I said.

Above us the boom boom of invisible forces.

*

Victor said, What I am about to say is undocumented and unknown. I imagine I can trust you?

You're sleeping with me, I said.

And you are sleeping with me, he said, but you do not trust me.

I was silent.

He seemed a little embarrassed by his sharpness.

Let's agree to trust each other on this, I said.

All right, said Victor. Well, then, before he died, Jack and I agreed that we would preserve his head.

His head?

His head. Yes. With a view to returning him to consciousness some day.

His head is at Alcor?

Correct. Jack had done so much work on machine intelligence. He jested about cryopreservation, though he remained unconvinced by it. But what was there to lose? And so we made our pact. He was curious about the coming world.

That world hasn't come yet, I said. The technology doesn't exist.

That is true, said Victor. But we must try.

Try what?

I am going to try to scan his brain.

Victor was standing under a flickering overhead neon light. His expression was fixed. His eyes fragmented blue as the light shadowed and illuminated him.

He said, Medical ethics don't allow any experiments on the human brain; the scanning technology is so invasive it results in death – but what if the person will die in any case? The terminally ill making a sacrifice for humanity. Why can't I work on that brain? The killer on Death Row could be offered the chance of a final act of reparation. I could scan his brain. What loss to the world is a serial killer?

Victor! Stop it!

He said, There is always loss, always failure. Don't you think these experiments are going on in secret, in other parts of the world? Where human life is cheap? And if a hostile power were to achieve this . . . Jesus – they have already modified an embryo in China. Without any oversight or protocol at all. Don't you think they are working on other things too?

This is madness, I said.

What is sanity? he said. Can you tell me? Poverty, disease, global warming, terrorism, despotism, nuclear weapons, gross inequality, misogyny, hatred of the stranger.

He's pacing, pacing, like a thing caged in its own body. A thing trapped in its own time.

He tried to calm himself. Steady himself. He said, Alcor can't release the head without a doctor in charge. I need you to go and get Jack and bring him back here. To Manchester. To my laboratory.

I can't do that, Victor.

Of course you can. It is legal. The paperwork is in place.

He moved towards me. I turned away. I said, Is this why you came after me? Is this what you realised you could use me for? When we met? Is this what it's been about all along? First grave-robber and now ferryman? To bring you the dead?

Victor looked at me. He didn't flinch. Ry, I am not using you. Please understand that.

That's not what it feels like to me.

Then how can I convince you?

Can we go now? I said. Out of here?

He is recovered. He is himself. He smiles at me. The flush goes out of his face. His eyes no longer light the room. He gets our coats. He holds mine for me while I put it on. Ordinary actions. Ordinary life.

Out now, out of the concrete and steel. Out of the harsh neon and deep shadows. Away from the machines. Away from the thud of suction pumps and the weight of water. Corridors, lino, stairs, leading up and up, and I am counting, sensing the air change, like a visitor leaving the underworld.

And then we're out in the rainy damp of the home-time rush, and he's locking the gates just as though we've been on one of those tours people love: Subterranean Secret of the City.

And no one cares or notices us. We could be invisible. Maybe we are invisible. He walks on as if nothing has happened, his hands in his trench-coat pockets, holding the undone coat around his body against the weather.

We walk in silence until we reach the corner where I will turn to walk to the station. Then I hesitate, and he can read my hesitation. I should have said goodbye and walked on.

He said, I know you were taking the train tonight, but stay, will you? Leave in the morning? I have to be up early myself.

I don't answer, but I fall into step with him, slower, trying to think, but at the same time seeking his reassurance, wanting to feel lighter and freer than I do. Wanting to turn away and take the train. Knowing that I won't.

A tram hoots as it rumbles past on metal rails.

Victor steps back; for a split second I imagined him stepping forward. My heart is beating too fast.

He is contrite. Not like himself. Looking straight ahead, he says, I said too much.

I don't answer. My mind is rioting but I don't answer him. I know how it is. Saying too much. Saying too little. Who says enough? Just enough?

My closest conversations are bad translations.

That's not what I meant – not what I meant at all.

I am so uncertain of what I can manage that the certainty of another person is like an oracle. Victor is certain. He takes the weight off me. But what is the weight in himself?

He puts his arm around me. He says, I am sorry. Can we lie down together? Won't you come home with me? Forget the rest. Forget it all.

Already we are crossing the street together, moving through this passing time and our own story.

Victor lives in an old warehouse on the top floor. Steel columns, exposed brick, long windows that open onto the roof of the city. His apartment is neat; forensically arranged. The colours are grey and brown with a vast red rug like a bloodstain. In the bedroom the big metal bed looks out onto a silent tower. The bell is still there, he says, but it never tolls.

He closes the blinds. The room smells of lavender and brandy. He sits on the bed to remove his boots. I sit on the other side with my back to him, picking up his bedside book – a biography of Robert Oppenheimer.

Am I in your light? he asks, turning on his knees and leaning over to me. He puts his arms around me. This is so simple, so clear, and nothing else is. I turn to kiss him, and I wish the moment could hold, that time could be anywhere but here.

Victor turns the pages of the book. Oppenheimer was many things . . . a brilliant physicist, a mystic, a man who never forgave himself for the atomic bomb. It is not always possible to forgive oneself. And sometimes you make a choice to do something, knowing that you must do it, and that forgiveness is impossible.

He undoes my shoes like a mother, and peels off my socks, my jeans, and then he leaves me in my shirt in the half-light while he goes into the kitchen to make some food, fetch some wine. I like the firm, clean feel of his bed.

His bed. He sends his sheets to the laundry. He prefers the crispness of starched cotton. He comes back in with a tray, and tumblers, a Chianti, and bruschetta with chopped fresh basil, tomatoes and garlic. He makes us a world when we are together like this. He takes trouble. He's kind. He gives me a napkin to put round my neck and feeds me small pieces of food as if I am a baby bird.

I take his hand in mine. Kiss it. Twist the gold ring on his little finger. I ask him, What's the imprint on your signet ring?

He shows me. A snake swallowing its own tail. He says, We come full circle. Whether we know it or not.

Then he pulls me to him on the bed.

His bed. Two square metres of safety.

His bed, where I don't need to explain. Where he doesn't give me his theories of everything. Where his eyes are calm and deep. In his bed there's his body and his desire.

He feels intimate. This is intimate. Our life raft. But if this is the raft, what is the shipwreck?

We are.

Differently disabled – his pessimism about love, my fear of it. Our wounded lives take shelter here. Why can't we mend ourselves? Why can't we save each other?

He kisses me, rests my face in his neck, runs his hand down my spine, his leg crossing mine. I love the warmth of his skin and the dark hair that tingles my fingers.

We make love without speaking. His hair falls into my face. Full of him, I forget my fear. The shadows recede.

Night deepens and he falls asleep above the noises of the city. The apartment is dark but for the two candles above the bed. I raise myself up to blow them out. He stirs and rolls over into his own private sleep. Check the clock. In a couple of hours I'll be finding my clothes in the dark and leaving for the train.

Yet this night feels like forever – not that it will last forever but that it is forever. This is where we belong. Our capsule lost in space. The rest is a dream we're dreaming. He talks in his sleep.

This night-soaked bed.

I lie back down quietly beside him and drift into his dark. Time will find us out but not yet. Enough to sleep in the temporary forever of now.

You know I am not born to tread in the beaten track – the peculiar bent of my nature pushes me on.

Mary Wollstonecraft

Bedlam 3

It was evening when she came, her hair the colour of copper, the sun on it like an Aladdin's lamp. There was something of the genie about her, quick and transparent of form, yet she held herself confidently and shook my hand.

He is here?
He is in my study.
He believes . . .
He believes that you created him.

Before I could say more, the door opened and Victor Frankenstein entered the room. The food and rest he has enjoyed in my care have restored him to health. He is handsome. She too. Their glances met. He held out his hand.

You are Mary Shelley.
I am she.
She was composed. Unafraid.
He turned to me eagerly and said, You have shown her my papers? All my papers?

She is acquainted with your credentials.

Yes. That is why I am here, she said.

I poured wine. I did not know what else to do. We sat down.

Unmake me, he said.

The lady gazed at him for some while. He appeared very far from mad, but very often the mad have a deep conviction the sane lack.

You have appeared in the pages of a novel, she said. You and the monster you created.

I am the monster you created, said Victor Frankenstein. I am the thing that cannot die – and I cannot die because I have never lived.

My dear sir! (At this I had to intervene.) If I were to shoot you now, with this pistol (I took the pistol from my pocket), your life would be at an end. Yes, sir! A dead end.

I pray you do it, Mr Wakefield, he said. If I leave this body, still I shall return. This form I show to you now is temporary. I exist for all time, unless my creator frees me.

I shook my head sadly. I had entertained hopes for him. Now I fear he will never leave this place. Poor delusionist!

Mary Shelley seemed unafraid of his wild claims. She said, Tell me, then, sir, how you have come out of the pages of a book, and into this life?

Victor Frankenstein said, There has been an error. I should have perished on the ice. Instead I find myself here, in this madhouse, and I know that he whom I loathe is loose in the world and seeks my destruction.

Yet you wish to die! I said.

I wish to disappear! I do not belong in this body. This gross body!

My husband would understand you there, sir, she said.

This body! he continued. I scarcely recognise it. I am Mind. Thought. Spirit. Consciousness.

Dear sir, be calm! I said. Do you not know that each of us fails to recognise our face in the mirror as time robs us of youth and vigour? Do you imagine I was always thus? (I gestured to my girth and gout.) I was a fencing champion, sir. A greyhound! No, no, each of us turns away in dismay from what he must become.

I have never been like you! answered the man. My madness is that I am trapped here. Outside waits one whose fiendish, pitiless cunning will instruct others to experiment as I did – without any care for the human race.

Mary Shelley said, If you are not of the human race, why should you care for it?

For the love of it that you bear, he answered. Love that you have taught me. Shall I quote our book? *My heart was fashioned to be susceptible of love and sympathy.*

She said, Those words are spoken not by Victor Frankenstein, but by his creature.

We are the same, the same, answered Frankenstein.

The lady paused then, as though remembering some thought of her own. She replied to him, If you are the same, then you too must be the pitiless fiend of infinite cunning.

215

And of sorrow, he said. And of sorrow.

The deep night surrounded us. The long candles in their holders had burned low. I wondered at us here, and what strangeness we met with. There are passages of time that tell more like text than time, when we sense we are a story we repeat, or a story that is told. What did he say? The teller or the tale? I do not know.

I drew her aside. I said to her, Madam, in my long association with the mad, I have heard many a lost soul who truly believes he is the Emperor of Russia or Alexander the Great or the mother of Christ, or Christ himself. The mind is a curious condition. An invention.

An invention? she said.

I do believe it, I said. By consent, the majority of us live and die as though the world around us is solid, even though each day disappears without trace. Our actions have consequences that rebound through time, yet each day disappears and a new day takes its place. The mad do not share our world. Their own is equally vivid. More so. The mad are actors on a different stage.

Mary Shelley drank wine. I like a woman who drinks wine, not sip sip sip but in a draught, like a mouthful of air. I said, This wine is from Cahors.

She said, I learned to drink wine in Italy, and I find it is excellent for the damp, for melancholy, and for writing.

Yes, indeed, I said. Your famous book. Such a stir!

216

You have read it?

Indeed!

The response of society was unexpected, she said, perhaps because I am a woman.

Your husband did not write it, then? As Sir Walter Scott assumes?

Shelley is a poet. He is Ariel, not Caliban. He did not write *Frankenstein*.

May I ask? Is your husband informed of your visit here?

He is attending to family matters, she said.

Our man sprang up and went to the window. He cried out: THERE! Do you see? He is there.

Who is there? I said.

The creature!

All three of us peered into the dark yard.

No one is there, I said.

If I am here, then he is there, replied Victor Frankenstein. That you cannot see him means nothing. You cannot see God but by his effects. Believe me, you will see his effects. The monster once made cannot be unmade. What will happen to the world has begun.

What terrified me will terrify others.

Mary Shelley

Reality is your hand on my heart.

This doesn't look like much of a place! said Ron Lord.

It's not the pyramids of Egypt. It's not a grove of cypress trees, or a sombre mausoleum built of hand-cut stone. There's no stained glass, no wrought-iron gates. No chapel of rest. No weeping angels, kneeling maidens, knights recumbent, faithful dogs, life-size likenesses, vases in which to leave flowers. Memorial stones. *In loving memory of.*

We're standing outside a concrete cube built on an out-of-town office and retail park near the runway of Scottsdale Airport, close to Phoenix. There's a tile warehouse in the next lot.

Welcome back to Alcor, Ry!
     Max More, the CEO, is waiting for us.
     Hi, Max! Good to see you again. Victor emailed you about Ron Lord, didn't he? Here he is: Ron Lord.
     (Hand-shaking all round.)

Ron! Good to meet you! Are you a friend of Victor Stein?

(How many of Victor's friends wear double-denim, tooled boots and a Stetson? Ron has dressed for his mini-break.)

I'm an investor, said Ron. I invest in the prof. I invest in the future.

You could invest in Alcor, said Max.

I might, said Ron. I get a lot of flak for what I do. You wouldn't believe the hostility at the cutting edge.

New is frightening, said Max.

Ron nodded. Yeah, you're right. I guess you get trouble too, what with this place freezing folks like TV dinners.

There is a lot of misunderstanding, said Max.

Same in my business, said Ron. Pioneers-R-Us.

Would you like to have a look around? said Max.

Is it creepy? said Ron. I don't look sensitive but I am sensitive.

We went inside the storage facility. The tall aluminium cylinders stood polished and reflective on their giant castors.

These are the dewars, said Max. Named after the inventor, Sir James Dewar. He came up with the idea in 1872.

What? said Ron, You saying they were freezing guys back in 1872?

I interrupted. Ron, what you see here are oversized thermos flasks. James Dewar was a Scot who invented the thermos flask; a vacuum between a double wall of steel coated with a reflective surface. Hot stays hot and cold stays cold.

Ron was frowning under his new cowboy hat. He said, You mean these are like the things I drink my coffee out of?

The very same.

Ron went over and tapped a dewar. He looked at me, touchingly puzzled. You mean there's people in here?

Yes, I said. Suspended head first, floating at minus 190 Celsius.

Ron removed his hat, out of respect.

Ryan, just explain. You're a doc. They go in dead, don't they?

Legally dead, yes.

What's legally dead?

It means your wife can spend all your money.

She did that while I was alive.

Well, ask yourself this question, Ron: what is death?

Don't get stupid on me, Ryan. Dead is dead.

Ron, there's a problem – but it isn't a problem with a comforting solution. Medically, and legally, death is deemed to occur at heart failure. Your heart stops. You take your last breath. Your brain, though, is not dead, and will not die for another five minutes or so. Perhaps ten or fifteen minutes in extreme cases. The brain dies because it is deprived of oxygen. It is living tissue like the rest of the body. It is possible that our brain knows we are dead before it dies.

Ron said, You're fucking with me.

I am not fucking with you, Ron.

Ron said, You're telling me that I will know I am dead and I will know there's nothing I can do about it?

I said, Very possibly. I am sorry.

Yeah, me too, said Ron.

I tried to cheer him up. (Probably people shouldn't talk about these things.) In the view of Alcor, death is not an event; death is a process. Correct, Max?

Correct, said Max, and Ron, if the brain can be preserved during the process we call death, perhaps it can be restored to consciousness some time in the future.

Ron seemed a bit more cheerful about this. OK! OK! I'm getting it! But if this is all about the brain, why all the fuss about the body? People are mostly old when they die, aren't they? And sick. So do they come back as sick, old people?

The theory, Ron, I said, is that smart medicine will be able to renew and reverse the aged body. On the other hand, by preserving the brain only, we may be able to grow, or to manufacture, a brand-new body. Or, if you listen to Victor, you won't need a body at all.

I don't fancy being a disembodied body, said Ron.

Come over here, Ron, said Max. These dewars that you see here are much smaller. This is where we store the heads.

Just heads?

Just heads . . .

So what do you do? Chop 'em off?

*

224

Cephalic isolation (or 'neuroseparation') is performed by surgical transection at the sixth cervical vertebrae.

Wow, said Ron. I suppose they have the best surgeons do the job?

Vets can do it. (Why do I tell him this? Am I evil?)

VETS! (Exclamation marks stream out of Ron's mouth.)

Yes, why not vets? The most interesting advances in vitrification have been on rabbits.

I am not letting a fuckin' vet saw off my head! says Ron. It's bad enough when I take Simba for his injections. I can't look!

You won't have to look.

What happens to my body afterwards?

Your family can cremate you.

Ron is staring at the dewars where the heads are kept.

Max, have they got their hair on?

Individual wishes are respected, says Max.

Funnily enough, says Ron, I have a factory of my own, in Wales, where we make heads – for my sexbots. In a way, we're in the same business. Alcor should expand in Wales. There'll be enterprise grants because of Brexit. Once the euro-millions is finally spent, there'll be nothing to do in Wales. You'll get tax breaks, warehousing, free fridges, free ice, maybe even vets. Whatever you want. Have you thought of franchising the business?

Max tells him that presently there are four cryonics facilities around the world – in the USA and in Russia.

Only four? says Ron. There's a gap in the market there.

There certainly is, Ron, I say, because 55 million people a year drop dead.

Ron considers this number carefully. Yeah, he says, we get a lot of no-shows on our Sexbot Subscription Plan. Usually turns out they're dead.

We also have a subscription plan, says Max.

Yeah, but your lot are expecting to be dead, says Ron. That's what they're paying for? Right?

Ron wanders away, hat in hand. It's all too much to take in for Ron, and his processing speed is having a bit of an outage.

What happens in a power cut? he says. That could be a drawback with Wales. Right in the middle of dinner, usually Thursdays. Bang! The electric goes off.

Max explains that the dewars are so cold that a temporary power loss doesn't matter. Even a few weeks wouldn't matter.

What if there's a nuclear war? asks Ron.

Max suggests there will be other things to worry about.

Ron sees the good sense of this. His processing speed picks up and he spots a pattern in the data.

Ryan, you just said that 55 million people die every year?

Yes . . .

We wouldn't want them all back though, would we?

Author's note: THIS IS THE MOST PROFOUND THING RON HAS EVER SAID.

*

I mean, says Ron, where do you draw the line? Murdering bastards, child molesters, thugs, nutters, that bloke in Brazil – Bolsonaro. What if you had Hitler's head in a bag in there? Would you defrost it? And then there's really boring people . . . And where are we all going to fit? On the planet, I mean?

Max reassures Ron that by the time the technology is functional we will soon be colonising the stars.

Is Donald Trump getting his brain frozen? asks Ron.

Max explains that the brain has to be fully functioning at clinical death.

I might freeze my mum, says Ron. She'd love to live on a star.

Max shows Ron the dewars where the pets live.

Do they keep their fur? asks Ron.

Max knows that fur is an important part of a pet, so he is able to reassure Ron. He also suggests cloning.

Is that expensive, Max?

Very.

I can afford it, says Ron. Actually I was about to say, you can't take it with you, but maybe you should! You drop dead. All the relatives spend your money, then bingo! You're back! Then what?

I have to say that at this moment I look at Ron with new respect. Who exactly is thinking about the nitty-gritty of the future, except Ron Lord?

*

And now Ron is really on a roll. The Alcor warehouse is having a profound effect on his brain. As we stand by the dewars and their suspended, pending occupants, Ron launches into a disquisition on the immortality of sexbots. A companion for our many lives.

You might return, and there she is, just as you remember, and she remembers you. I mean, Max, I mean, this is something we should be thinking about together. I'm looking for partnerships. I don't mean intimate partnerships, I mean business partnerships. This could be for your clients. A sexbot is better than a widow.

Partners can both come back together, says Max. Even if they die twenty years apart.

Ron is shaking his head and cowboy hat. This isn't cutting it for him.

Listen, says Ron. Listen! I've learned a thing or two in my business. Now that people are living longer, marriages don't work as well as they used to. People need a change. If I'm coming back, I might not want the missus, and she might not want me. Better to start with a bot-u-like, and see how it goes.

Wouldn't you like to fall in love, Ron? I say.

Ryan, I know you think you're smart, but let me tell you something about relationships. Most of the people, most of the time, are in horrible relationships, dreaming about being in a good relationship. And it's a fantasy. It's like the beach body you'll never have – not counting you, Max, because I can see you're pretty ripped under that T-shirt. Most men look like me . . . Ryan! Shut up!

228

You don't count. So I say, face the facts, Max, and get your subscription plan to include a sexbot.

At that moment the door to the storage facility opened and a tall, beautiful black woman walked in. I recognised her immediately. It was Claire from Memphis.

Claire! How are you?

You two know each other? said Max.

Yes! No! I said. We met in Memphis.

We surely did, said Claire. Quite an experience.

What? At the sex show? said Ron. Were you a hostess?

I was facilitating, said Claire, as icy as the North Pole.

Is that more high class? said Ron.

Sir! I was not part of the entertainment programme.

No offence meant, said Ron.

What are you doing here? I said.

I am Max More's personal assistant.

Well, that's a change.

Yes, it is.

I'd love to hear about it, I said. Would you like to come for a drink later?

I might do that, Dr Shelley, said Claire.

Can I come? said Ron.

And that is how we wound up at a little bar with a tin roof and a wide porch and a pretty girl wearing a TAKE IT EASY T-shirt, in the matter-of-fact mystery of the Sonoran Desert.

Welcome back! she said.

You been here before as well? said Ron.

In a previous life. That's what it feels like, I said.

Do you believe in reincarnation? said Claire.

The waitress said, When he was last here, he drank bourbon and he ate melted cheese. Shall I bring some?

The waitress sashayed away.

That is a beautiful ass, said Ron.

Women are not body parts! said Claire.

How is a man supposed to give a woman a compliment, then? said Ron. You a #MeToo type?

I won't get into my politics, said Claire, I'll just tell you that you can say the following to a woman: what intelligent eyes she has. What a beautiful soul she has. What deep understanding she has. What fine dress sense she has.

Is that all? said Ron.

Think of it like practising the piano, said Claire. Get those right and we can try some other pieces.

Ron looked impressed. He said, Can I buy you a drink?

Ryan is buying me a drink, said Claire.

He's called Mary, said Ron.

Pardon me?

I decided to interrupt this moment of Ron-ness.

Claire! Tell me, how did you get from the World Barbecuing Championship to Alcor? It's quite a step.

Yes, it is, Ry (she said my name with some emphasis while ice-staring Ron). I had a vision.

A vision?

From the Lord.

Claire started to sing ROCK OF AGES, CLEFT FOR ME/LET ME HIDE MYSELF IN THEE. She had a great voice. The table near us clapped.

I am here undercover, said Claire. As an envoy of my Family in the Lord. I am hidden in the cleft of the rock to discover the Soul.

Whose soul? I said.

The Souls of the Departed! said Claire. If you die. If you are vitrified. If you return to life here on earth in this Vale of Tears, tell me this: where is your Soul?

That's a thought, said Ron. Where is it?

My question is this, said Claire: will the Soul return to the Self, or has the Soul gone to Jesus? Permanently?

How are you going to find out? I asked.

I have no idea, said Claire. But I was told by the Lord to come here, and, taking a pay cut, I did. The thing is, I hold different views to some others in my church because I might believe in reincarnation.

Might you? I said.

Claire nodded her beautiful head. (I am not supposed to say her beautiful head, am I? OK. Claire nodded her head that contained her intelligent eyes.)

Maybe, Ry, we have to consider that returning a person to life is an update on reincarnation.

Right! said Ron. (Claire glared at him.)

So if we come back, our Soul should join us, surely it should?

I hope so, I said.

And that Soul would be part of your past life, said Claire, a Soul refining itself through another life.

231

Don't you want to be Saved? I said.

I am Saved! said Claire. My salvation is mine for eternity. My current job at Alcor is to ascertain whether Christian people should get themselves vitrified so that when they return to this Tormented Land of Sin, they can testify, without a doubt, that while their heads were on ice, their Soul was with Christ.

Wow! said Ron. You are quite a lady.

I will take that as a compliment, Ron, said Claire, graciously.

The problem is, Claire, I said, that you might be working at Alcor for a long time. Possibly past retirement age, because the technology is years away.

There could be a breakthrough, said Claire. And at least I am gaining knowledge. Not many people understand cryonics.

I am a bit surprised by this move of yours, I said, because, when we spoke in Memphis, you were dead against robotics.

Yes, I am against robots, said Claire. But I have to make up my mind about the future on a case-by-case basis. What is from God? And what is from the Devil?

You think robots are from the Devil? I said.

Robots can be used by the Devil, said Claire, to undermine the sanctity of being human.

Can I say something? said Ron.

The waitress came over with the grilled cheese and the bourbon. She said, We have a steel-string band tonight. Guitars, banjo, ukulele. Enjoy!

Miss, do you believe in reincarnation? I said.

The waitress sat sideways on the edge of my chair. I could feel the length of her leg against mine. She said, Y'know, I really do. I know I have been here before. On this earth. It's hard to talk about. It's really a deep feeling you have. A vision of the past.

I had a vision – said Ron – it's how I started my business. Did you see my exhibition stand at the Sexpo, Claire? The one with the purple curtains? It was called Waiting For The King.

You're not a king, said Claire.

No, I'm not, said Ron, and most men are not kings, but with a little lady made just for you, it's different.

Wait a minute . . . you sell sexbots, said Claire, slowly, like remembering a bad dream.

Yes! said Ron.

That is disgusting, said Claire.

Ron pushed his hat to the back of his head. He leaned forward and looked Claire straight in her (intelligent) eyes.

Let me tell you something, said Ron. I was brought up in Welsh Chapel. My mum is a Sunday-school teacher. Do you want to know what my business motto is?

No, said Claire.

Judge Not That Ye Be Not Judged, said Ron. Matthew Chapter 7.

Claire said, We are obliged to take a moral stance . . . we—

But Ron interrupted her. Motes and beans, Claire.

What? I said, wondering at this latest Ron-ish.

233

He means beams, not beans, said Claire.

It says in the Bible, said Ron, that we should stop yakking about the mote – that's a speck, right, in our mate's eye – and take a look at the bean, or beam or whatever, in our eye. Right, Claire?

That is what the Bible says, yes, agreed Claire, reluctantly.

Well, then, said Ron, take a look in the mirror, Claire. I'm not the one lying to my employer, and acting like a Russian spy! I am the one providing a service to people in need. Do you realise what sexbots could do for the Catholic Church? All those priests with erections under their man-skirts? With a bot behind the altar there'd be no need to abuse orphans and choirboys. There'd be no adultery, no fornication, none of that stuff in Exodus about shagging your brother's wife.

I feel ill, said Claire. Excuse me, please!

She got up to go but Ron held up his hand.

Hear me out! said Ron. And when you've heard me out, judge me if you want to.

Claire sat down. I passed her the grilled cheese. She ate it mechanically (I was about to say robotically, but bots don't eat). She ate it like a woman who needs help, even if it is from mozzarella.

Ron said, When my wife kicked me out – couldn't happen with a bot – could not happen – I had to go back to live with my mum, but I couldn't get in with any of the locals. I'd go down the pub and they'd all turn their backs and start speaking Welsh. I was an outsider and everyone was married.

So I bought myself a love-doll. Yes, I did. Mail-order. She was basic but she was mine.

I have always been a lonely man.

A sexbot is not a human being! said Claire.

That's right! said Ron. And neither is a dog or a cat. We wouldn't be without them, though, would we? Even tropical fish! People can feel close to fish. They come home from work and sit next to the aquarium. We all need something. That's life. So why not a robot? My first bot was there for me when I got home from work and there was none of the usual *where have you been what time do you call this?* She was ready in bed for a cuddle, and I was getting sex every night. No warm-up. Straight in. Slept with my arm across her. I felt better. Stopped the Xanax. My rash cleared up.

(I glanced at Claire. Her intelligent eyes were fixed on Ron. She was mesmerised. Maybe Ron has something after all.)

Then a mate of mine back in Essex got made redundant and he said he was going to put his packet into Bitcoin. We had a look at it together online, and I thought I'd give it a go with the money that was mine when the divorce came through. Mum had been hoping for a new bathroom suite but what can you do?

I put in five large, and a year later, guess what? £300,000 in real money.

Mum got her bathroom suite. 'Course she did. And a new kitchen. Then she said to me, Daffodil! (She calls me Daffodil because I wear aftershave.) She said, Go on holiday, Daffodil, you deserve it.

I said, Where shall I go, Mum? And she fell into a bit of a trance, because she's a bit psychic, my mum, and she said, Thailand! Something is waiting for you there.

So, out in Thailand there was this woman offering sexbots for sex. Very crude bots made in Korea – and not well-washed – and I didn't want to do it with them anyway, even for free – they were offering the first shag free – because I didn't want to spoil what I had with my own bot-girl at home. So I went with regular prostitutes. Lovely girls. Most of 'em still at school. I don't judge – it's a different style over there.

I was helping one with her English homework every night. I write poetry. That will surprise you, Ryan, but I do.

And I felt sorry for those girls – I really did, because some of the blokes out there need to soak their dicks overnight in a bottle of bleach.

Then – and this is how it happened – this is it coming up now. I was out one night under the stars – millions of them, like winning the silver-dollar jackpot off the slot machines at Vegas. Stars pouring out of the sky.

Then, with no warning, there was this big electric storm – big as God.

I was nervous because I'd just had my dick pierced for a bet, and I thought, suppose my dick gets struck by lightning?

I stood hovering in the darkness waiting for disaster. The resort I was staying in was shut down in total blackness, and I couldn't find my way back, and I thought, even if I don't get struck by lightning, this could be the end of the world. And I've done nothing with my life. Repaired a few toasters, and that's more or less it.

I didn't move. I was like a dead man. Your life flashes before you, flash, flash, because there's so little of it. I mean, what have you ever done that was worth doing? I think what was happening to me was religious because later on, at home, I talked about it to the Reverend and he said, *Daffodil, you were standing on a vast plain of emptiness.*

Then I had a vision.

I saw armies of lonely men walking along a ruined road. Men with their heads bowed and their hands in their pockets. Nobody was talking. Each one walked alone.

Then, coming towards the men, suddenly, down the same ruined road, were all these beautiful girls. Girls who would never get old or ill. Girls who would always be saying *yes* and never saying *no*.

And in the sky there was the moon, big as a Bitcoin, and I knew I had to put myself at the service of human-kind.

But there's only so much you can do in Wales.

That's why I've gone global.

Ron sat back. Claire was staring at him. She said, You were sent to me tonight.

You reckon? said Ron.

Claire said, I believe in your vision, Ron. I believe it was real.

Thanks, said Ron.

But you have put your vision in the service of Satan! Not humankind . . . Satan. Lust is one of the Seven Deadly Sins!

Men will always want women, said Ron quietly.

Claire's eyes were shining. Have you ever thought of manufacturing a doll for Jesus?

Do you think he wants one? asked Ron.

I am talking about a Christian Companion, said Claire. Yes! It's coming to me now! For the missionary, for the widower, for the boy tempted by the flesh. A Sister in Christ who could also . . .

Fuck you? said Ron.

That is a little crude, said Claire. I have an MBA, by the way, in Management.

Claire! Wait! I said. I thought you were here to investigate the future of our souls. Now you want to partner up with Ron in the bot business?

I go where the Lord leads me, said Claire, and I believe that my Lord has led me to Ron Lord.

238

They certainly share a surname, I said.

(Now it's me Claire is glaring at.)

There's something I want to tell you, said Ron. I hope you won't be offended.

Go ahead.

My first sexbot, really, I suppose, the love of my life, was called Claire. That is, I called her Claire. She's retired now. But, well, to me, sitting here now, it's like you have come back to me in human form.

I was only suggesting I take a look at your spreadsheets, said Claire.

Yeah, yeah, said Ron, but this is sorta like a vision as well, isn't it?

It may well be a gift from the Lord, said Claire. Tell me, how do you dress your bots?

Ron got out his phone. Please note that this is for the Adult market, Claire, not for Jesus.

Claire was flicking through Ron's portfolio of leather and lace, denim and Lycra, thongs and tassels.

What I have in mind, said Claire, is a neat dress, tied-back hair, nice skin, no make-up, and—

Would we have to shrink the cup-size? said Ron.

40F might be a little too large for the Christian Companion, said Claire.

It would have to be specialist production, said Ron, like my Outdoor Girl. She's the one that I do in partnership with Caterpillar. I mean, if I am going to invest in a new model, I'd have to be sure there's a market.

We will create a market, said Claire with surprising ruthlessness. That's how business works.

That's how late capitalism works, I said.

Are you a communist, Ry? said Claire. I am a member of the Republican Party. A strong economy works for everyone.

No, it doesn't, I said. But I am not a communist.

He's trans, said Ron. Like I said, his real name is Mary.

My 'real' name is not Mary!

Claire didn't look pleased. She didn't sound pleased either . . . I am shocked at you, Dr Shelley. God makes us as we are and we should not tamper with it.

I said, If God hadn't wanted us to tamper with things She wouldn't have given us brains.

I agree with him on that, said Ron. Which is unusual. No offence, Claire.

I can see there is a lot of work for me to do here, said Claire. Yes, I can see that THE Lord led me to Alcor for this meeting tonight. I have found my mission.

Let me pour you another drink, said Ron.

Claire, what's it like to be so certain about everything? I said. I mean, one minute you hate bots, and they're all part of Satan's plan to enslave humanity, and now you want to partner with a sexbot king.

Claire looked at me with compassion (or contempt?). Ryan, man proceeds by the arrogance of his intellect and his ego. I follow the path of revelation and inspiration. I change my mind when the Lord tells me to change my mind.

OK, I said, I get it. But tell me, Claire, don't you ever hesitate? Doubt? Cry alone at night for what you can't understand about yourself – or others?

No, said Claire. I pray. And I will pray for you, Mary. No one in the Bible is trans.

The Bible was a long time ago, Claire, I said. No one in the Bible flies in a plane, drinks bourbon or eats grilled cheese. Or . . . straightens their hair with hot tongs.

You have lovely hair, said Ron

Everything changes, said Claire. I change. You change. God changes not.

The band came back on stage. Good beat. Good tunes. Claire pulled Ron to his feet and challenged him to a square dance. I got up to find the restroom. It was a little way down the back of the bar, outside under the stars, in a set of stalls. The music faded as I pushed through the swing doors.

There was a guy at the urinal, older, heavy, unsteady on his feet. I glanced at him and went into a cubicle. I heard him finishing up. He heard me peeing. He kicked the door and shouted, YOU THINK I'M A FAGGOT?

I ignored him. A second later he had crashed out of the restroom, the door swinging back and forth. I zipped up, came out, and was washing my hands when he crashed back in. WHAT'S SO PRECIOUS ABOUT YOUR FUCKIN' COCK THAT YOU KEEP IT TO YOURSELF?

You're drunk, I said. Leave me alone.

I went towards the door. He blocked my way, his eyes swimming with drink. PISS LIKE A MAN. GO ON!

I'm done, I said. Excuse me, will you?

He mimicked me: EXCUSE ME, WILL YOU? You talk like a girl.

He lunged at my crotch – and found what I don't have.

WHAT THE FUCK?

Let me go, I said.

You're in the wrong stall, sonny, eh? What are you? A fuckin' dyke?

I'm trans.

He was shifting from foot to foot. Get in the stall! Since you like it in there.

I tried to move past him to leave. He rammed me so hard I lost my balance. I was on the floor. He reached down to drag me up.

I thought: I'm going to get beaten up or raped. Which is worse?

I didn't have to make that decision because he pushed me into the stall, slammed the door shut and forced me up against it. He fumbled with his zip and pulled his dick out, wanking himself half-hard.

THIS IS THE REAL DEAL YOU FUCKIN' DYKE FAGGOT. YOU WANT IT?

No.

You're getting it anyways. He pushed his hand under my shirt.

YOU FUCKIN' FREAK! YOU HAD YOUR TIT SLASHED OFF? NO TITS. NO DICK. FUCKIN' FREAK!

He started pulling at my jeans. His fat, dirty fingers were trying to get the zip down.

Get your hands off me, I said.

YOU DON'T LIKE MY HANDS ON YOU, YOU
LITTLE FREAK?

He hit the side of my face with the back of his fist.

DROP THEM, I SAID!

His face was an inch away from mine. He was
breathing cigarettes and whisky in my face. I undid my
jeans and turned my head away from him. I could feel
the blind, dead nub of his cock against my pubic hair.

He couldn't come. Kept dry-pumping and couldn't
come. He was a lot taller than me and twice as heavy,
but in the clarity that fear can bring I thought I could
unbalance him. Use his weight and his drunkenness
against him. He was so drunk he was resting his head
against the cubicle door while he shoved his way in.

OPEN YOUR FUCKIN' LEGS WIDER!

I moved, and as he moved I took a chance and pushed
him as hard as I could. He fell back against the toilet,
falling down, banging his head on the concrete wall. He
was stunned for a second, and away from the door
enough for me to get out. I pulled up my jeans, and ran
into the night behind the bar.

Outside, I stood still and quiet, fixing my clothes, feeling
myself carefully. No rips, no blood, no sperm. The dirty
smell of him on my fingers. He was coming out now,
lumbering, stumbling, shouting obscenities, angry. He
paused in the outside door, the shadow of him on the
deck. My sweat went cold. If he found me now . . . but
two other guys were heading for the restroom; I heard

their voices, their boots, then, HEY! STEADY, BUDDY! THAT'S THE WAY BACK TO THE BAR!

They must have turned him around because I heard the blast of music as he opened the door.

It's OK. It's OK, I said to myself.

I let myself slide down the rough wall of the outside shack. Knees under my chin. Folded into my own body. I was aching and sore. I needed a douche of disinfectant. Some cream. This isn't the first time. It won't be the last. And I don't report it because I can't stand the leers and the jeers and fears of the police. And I can't stand the assumption that somehow I am the one at fault. And if I am not at fault, then why didn't I put up a fight? And I don't say, try working on the Accident and Emergency unit for a few nights and see where putting up a fight gets you. And I don't say the quickest way is to get it over with. And I don't say, is this the price I have to pay for . . .?

For . . . For what? To be who I am?

Cry at night for what you can't understand in yourself or others. Cry at night. Don't you?

The tears make my knees wet as I sit with my face on my legs as small as I can make myself. Make myself. This is who I am.

What is your substance,
whereof are you made?

Hope is a duty. Hope is our reality.

Shelley says so and he believes it so, but for me the light has gone out. The light inside and the light outside. I have no lantern and no lighthouse. I am at sea in waves too high and the rocks wreck me.

Rome. Venice. Livorno. Florence. We have returned to Italy because we cannot live in England. Small-minded, smug, self-righteous, unjust, a country that hates the stranger, whether that stranger be a foreigner or an atheist, or a poet, or a thinker, or a radical, or a woman. For women are strange to men.

But that is not my darkness. My darkness is what it has been since I was born to it; the darkness of death.

My little daughter caught a fever. My husband had travelled to Venice and I made the decision to follow him when I should have stayed and nursed my child in quiet. Four days of carriages, dust, filth, rattle, noise, polluted water, and by the time I reached Venice and he ran for the doctor my beautiful Ca had stopped breathing in my arms. I would not give her up. I held her cooling body to me. What is there to say?

The following year, 1819, we were in Rome. My boy, Will – Willmouse, we have always called him – spoke Italian like a street seller. Italy is home to him.

We were warned not to stay in Rome. Malaria is deadly in the summer. But Will was happy there, and my spirits were returning, and my love for Shelley was strong enough to light the lantern in me again, and him my lighthouse.

And then it happened. I should have died on 7 June 1819. Instead, Willmouse died, a little each day for a week, until he was gone. The life of him, gone. Where does it go? This life that is so strong? Is that all? The chemistry and electricity once extinguished, where does the life go? I SAID, WHERE DOES THE LIFE GO?

My husband endeavoured to hold me, to stop me shouting at the painting on the wall. The painting of my child takes no fever. I am twenty-two years old. I have lost three children.

Shelley too, you will say, Shelley too, has lost three children. Yet he does not break. I am broken.

*

I am pregnant again. The next baby will be born in December. I do not know if I can bear this reality. The reality of death. Birth followed by death. Shelley comes to me: *Don't touch me.*

I see him hurt and rejected by my unkindness. Oh, my love, my lighthouse that I cannot see, I am not unkind. I am going mad. Do you hear me? (This woman shouting at the wall.) I AM GOING MAD.

Can't work, can't eat, can't sleep, can't walk, can't think, except in jagged flashes that show me in a graveyard among burial plots. When I dream I dream of dead children. Monsters. What have I created that I have killed?

I will not let the servants change the linen in the bed where he died in my arms. For three months I have lain in the stink of death. Is it preferable to rot by increments, as adults do, finally decaying to busy infested dust, or is it preferable to die as children do? Their bloom on their cheeks? Lips red. Oh, with faces so pale!

Take me away take me away take me away from death.

One morning in September, Shelley knocked at my door holding a letter and some pages of newspapers sent from England.

There has been a massacre, he said. A month ago, but the news has only reached us now. I have the reports here.

Where? I said.

In Manchester. In St Peter's Field. They are calling it Peterloo, after Waterloo.

I knew from my own experience how terrible were the conditions in Lancashire. In 1805 a weaver could earn fifteen shillings for a six-day week and keep his family without fear. In 1815, when the wars with Napoleon ended (and the wars ended with the Battle of Waterloo), those same workers might earn five shillings at best. In response, the government brought in the Corn Laws, forbidding the import of cheaper foreign grain to feed the starving families.

Why such madness? They called it patriotism. England for the English! John Bull bread at John Bull prices. The truth was other; the Corn Laws are for the benefit of fat gentleman farmers in England, at patriotic liberty to charge what they like for their corn. Thus they maintain their fortunes by starving women and children and by ruining working men. Such is that which we call government in England.

Well said, my love! said Shelley, heartened to see something of my natural sensibility appear before him. And it is true that I sat up in bed.

But what has happened to provoke this violence? I asked.

He came and sat on the edge of the bed.

He said, A meeting was called of the men and women of Lancashire to hear the radical orator Henry Hunt speak to them. The demands were to repeal the Corn Laws, so that honest men and women might eat as well as work, and to petition for an end to rigged parliaments, where MPs are elected out of the favouritism of the gentry and the aristocracy. The great manufactory towns and cities have no true representation.

That is correct, I said, for the wealth of England is shifting from the land to the towns, and yet these swelling numbers in the manufactories have no voice of their own, and none to speak on their behalf.

Indeed, indeed! said Shelley. It says so here, exactly that, in the newspaper. And according to the reports here (he held up the paper, for the print is small, and his eyes are weak), the meeting saw a great crowd – upwards of 100,000!

100,000! I said.

Yes, yes, he replied, and by all accounts sober and neatly dressed and orderly.

Then what was the provocation? I said.

Ah, well, said Shelley, instead of recognising the force of the protest, the magistrates sent in militias and, worse still, the dragoons on horseback with sabres, to break up what they called 'the mob', though all reports say the protestors were as calm as a church service.

This is wickedness, I said. And not wickedness of the people.

Shelley examined the newspaper: fifteen or twenty people were killed. Hundreds injured. It would appear that the dragoons particularly ran at the women.

Brave men! I said.

Shelley said, There has been a great outcry against the treatment of the protestors. The government is blaming them, and taking no responsibility for the actions of the Manchester magistrates, or for their own actions, that have led to this protest. Yet the outcry cannot be quieted. The very stones cry out!

Is it the beginning of revolution in England? I said.

I do not know, said Shelley. We shall have more news.

Would that my mother had seen this, I said. She would have travelled to Manchester.

We could return to England, said Shelley. To join our force to the protest.

I am pregnant, I said.

He took my hand. I know . . .

And then he said, Please come back to me, Mary. You are the soul of my Soul.

I held his hand, so pale and thin and long. That hand on my body, that hand in my hair, that hand feeding me cheese (my craving when I am with child), that hand writing out poems. His hand with the ring on his finger that tells the world he is my husband.

I have not left you, I said. (But it is not true.)

We can go to Florence, he said. Begin again.

We are always beginning again, I said. And do we leave a dead child behind in every place?

He jumped off the bed, covering his face, pacing to the window. He threw back the shutters. The light seemed to shine through him, spirit that he is.

Stop it, Mary! I implore you! Get up. Wash your face. Write! Write!

He strode back to me, took both my hands in his, and kneeled by the bed. My love, let us go to Florence. Our new baby will be born there.

In winter, I said.

In winter, he repeated. (Pausing, pausing.)

Then he said, If winter comes, can spring be far behind?

All those things we did. I rose. I had the servants soak the bedding in salt water. I bathed. I sat at my desk with a jug of wine and I inked my pen.

Frankenstein was published last year in England, and has had some success. It may live on. The strange part is that *his* face is in my dreams too. Victor. The Victor with no victory. Was it a coincidence that I wrote only of loss and failure?

I have been with Shelley for five years. During four of those years my children – surely the fruit of our life together – have been born and died. Is it punishment, after all, for the way we have lived? Outsiders and strangers.

My mother was not afraid to be an outsider. Yet she longed for love.

I have love, but I cannot find love's meaning in this world of death. Would there were no babies, no bodies; only minds to contemplate beauty and truth. If we were not bound to our bodies we should not suffer so. Shelley says that he wishes he could imprint his soul on a rock, or a cloud, or some non-human form, and when we were young I felt despair that his body would disappear, even though he remained. But now all I see is the fragility of bodies; these caravans of tissue and bone.

At Peterloo, if every man could have sent his mind and left his body at home, there could have been no massacre. We cannot hurt what is not there.

Imagine if there was no 'there' there? If we were the pure spirit of eternity, not bound to the wheels of death or time?

What if my Willmouse had been a spirit, able to put his body on and off as he pleased? No infection could have taken him. Our bodies could be like suits of clothes, while our minds run free. Where, then, would death find a home, if not in us? In my dreams my children call to me to come with them, just one turn more down the dark corridor. And I would go but for this life I carry.

A little patience, and all will be over.
My mother's last words upon her deathbed.

In Florence we lodge in a fine house. Shelley is reading *The History of the Rebellion and Civil Wars in England*, by Clarendon, and Plato's *Republic*. He is eager for a Republic of England. He never gives up his optimism – and I once shared it – now it seems to be that in the battle between good and evil, evil wins. Even our best endeavours turn against us. A loom that can do the work of eight men should free eight men from servitude. Instead, seven skilled men are put out of work to starve with their families, and one skilled man becomes the unskilled minder of the mechanical loom. What is the point of progress if it benefits the few while the many suffer?

I said this to Shelley as he read aloud, and frankly there is a limit to being read aloud to, especially when there is no wine in the house. The servant let the flagon fall off the donkey. Or she stole it.

I said to my husband, The many or the few?

He looked up. He ceased to read aloud. Mary! You have held me there. I am writing a poem about Peterloo. A poem of revolution and liberty and I want it read to men and women everywhere who are brave enough to demand freedom.

Have we got any cheese? I said.

My poem is called *The Masque of Anarchy*, said Shelley. Do you know what I read about myself in the library today? In the *Quarterly Review*? They had it just in from England. I was sitting in the English section, near that large woman with small eyes who goes to church every day and stares at us in the market. She was reading the *Review* also . . .

Mr Shelley would abolish the rights of property. He would overthrow the constitution . . . no army, no navy, he would pull down our churches, level our Establishment, marriage he cannot endure, and there would be a lamented increase of adulterous connections . . .

He recited from memory his list of misdemeanours. Finally he exclaimed, I would never pull down a church! I adore churches. It is what happens inside them that I detest.

Read to me your poem, instead of this recital of fear and envy from others, I said.

My poem is not ready, he said, but you have given me my best lines! Oh, Mary, do you remember, for I remember it, like a dog who scratches in despair on the door of an abandoned house where his master once lived, do you remember that summer in Geneva, when we worked together? You had begun writing *Frankenstein*, and oft we talked late into the night. Oft, I read to you from a new poem. We were happy.

Willmouse was alive, I said dreamily (for I did remember; how could I forget?).

Were we different then? he said. Are we those people?

He raised himself from his armchair and kissed my forehead.

Read to me, I said.

And so he began to read *The Masque of Anarchy*. And I listened to his voice going in and out like the sea, and I wondered, what will become of the human dream? Will we see it end in pain and despair? Will we be free from the brutality of this life? By some artful intelligence find a better way?

> 'Let the horsemen's scimitars
> Wheel and flash, like sphereless stars
> Thirsting to eclipse their burning
> In a sea of death and mourning.

> 'Stand ye calm and resolute,
> Like a forest close and mute,
> With folded arms and looks which are
> Weapons of an unvanquished war. . .

Shelley paused, writing with his pencil. I am putting in your lines, he said, modified to my purpose. This will be the final stanza.

> 'Rise like lions after slumber
> In unvanquishable number—
> Shake your chains to earth like dew
> Which in sleep had fallen on you—
> Ye are many—they are few.'

We are many, he said. Many Shelleys, many Marys. Many stand behind us tonight in spirit, and we shall do the same when we are done here. The body that must fail and fall is not the end of the human dream.

The human dream . . .

The Brain—is wider than the Sky—

Emily Dickinson

The steel box stood on the steel table.

Talking Heads! said Ron. I love that band. *True Stories*! Fantastic album. Did you see the movie? That fat guy who comes on singing 'I'm wearing fur pyjamas'. That's me.

There have been a number of talking heads in history, said Victor. That is, in the history of the human imagination. One of the strangest is attributed to the natural philosopher and part-time alchemist Roger Bacon. In the late 1200s, it seems he made a bronze head that could speak.

What did it say?

Very little: *Time Is. Time Was. Time is Past.* Then it exploded.

Time wasted, if you ask me, said Ron. My girls can talk a lot better than that – and they've got the health-and-safety Kitemark. Don't want your dick blown to bits, do you?

*

RON! said Claire. What did we agree about coarse and crude language?

Sorry, Claire, said Ron, contrite. Prof, I didn't introduce you yet – this is Claire, my new business partner and the love of my life. Claire, this is Professor Stein. He's a genius.

Thank you, Ron.

I'm putting a new bot into production called the Christian Companion. Claire has already emailed every evangelical church in the USA. We've had a fantastic response, haven't we, Claire?

Yes, we have! said Claire. The narrow road can be a lonely life. Jesus himself had his Mary Magdalene.

Didn't they have loads of children when they ran away to France? The Jesus and Mary Chain? Like in *The Da Vinci Code*? said Ron.

Theirs was a pure union, said Claire. Don't believe everything you read in Dan Brown.

Nice idea though, said Ron. Better than dying on the cross.

RON!

I mean, from Jesus's point of view . . .

Jesus died for our sins, Ron.

I know he did, Claire. I hear you. I'm just sorry he didn't make it to France.

Victor said, There are some theologians – as well as Dan Brown – who believe that Jesus had another life – a life that included children.

Jesus never, ever had sex, said Claire.

Are you sure? said Victor.

Positive, said Claire.

But Claire, said Ron, with our Christian Companion, I thought we agreed we were leaving the back and front holes open and fully vibrating? And the mouth . . .

We are, said Claire. Individual use is up to the individual.

Phew! said Ron. I've just put in an order for 20,000 God-bots. I don't want to be stoppering up 60,000 holes.

RON!

Sorry, Claire. You're the boss of my soul but business is business. Hey, Prof! Have you got a contact at the Vatican?

I'm afraid not, Ron. Besides, I thought you weren't interested in making boy-bots?

I wasn't, but that was because of the thrust. The new ones I have in mind aren't for the ladies. They are Service Bots. For the clergy. As long as the bum-hole is deep enough . . .

RON!!!!!

We have discussed this, sweetheart, said Ron. We agreed it would help vulnerable young people.

I just don't like talking about it with someone I've only just met, said Claire.

Oh, you can say anything to the prof, said Ron. He's a scientist.

Why don't we all have a cup of tea? said Victor. And then I must attend to my head.

It's a bit weird, said Ron. A head in a flask on the table. But this whole place is a bit weird.

*

The four of us were in the tunnels. The electrical supply was erratic that morning – bursts of jagged white illumination from the swinging lengths of strip lighting, then the insect-buzz of current fault and the on-off-on-off of now you see it, now you don't as we were split second in darkness, split second in cavern-light that seemed to watch us, not light us.

Claire was looking at two enormous generators the size of steam engines. Why are they called Jane and Marilyn? she asked.

The men who worked here during the Cold War named them after Marilyn Monroe and Jane Russell, said Victor. If you walk around here there are quite a few faded posters of 1950s movie stars.

They had amazing bodies back then, said Ron. It all went wrong with Twiggy. I blame crispbread.

Quite right, Ron, said Victor. Changes in diet can be blamed for most things. It will be interesting to see how non-biological life forms find ways to ruin themselves. It won't be sugar or alcohol or drugs.

I thought AI was going to be perfect? said Ron.

Who knows? said Victor. What have humans ever created that is perfect? We start with the best intentions . . .

You're selling this a bit differently than usual, Victor. This isn't your TED talk.

Victor shrugged. We shall find out. In any case, could it be worse than human? I read today that humans have wiped out sixty per cent of animal wildlife since 1970. In Brazil we have a dictator posing as a democratically elected president who is opening up the Amazon to commercial interests. Human beings really don't have a better chance than AI. We are too late for anything else.

What about the bloke in the box? said Ron. Isn't it too late for him?

The steel box stood on the steel table like the last challenge on a TV game show. *Open the box, Victor.*

I have something for Jack, if I succeed. Would you like to see?

Victor disappeared into one of his anterooms. Rooms I have never been invited into. Rooms like Bluebeard's chambers. One will be the smallest door with the bloodied key. But which one?

Victor returned with what looked like a cross between a puppet and a robot. The cylinder base ran on wheels. Above was a body with arms and a head. The whole thing was about 2 feet tall.

Jack was a small man, said Victor. I think he will like this. It's his new body.

You putting his brain in that? said Ron. It's like a toy for kiddies.

Not his brain. His brain is wetware. I won't need it when I have uploaded the contents. The brain is packaging. Think of yourself as data, Ron. Your data can be stored in many containers. At present it is stored in a large meat-safe.

Thanks, said Ron.

What I want to do is allow Jack to move around. One of the challenges of uploading a human is the shock they will experience at being out of a body. A body is what we know.

I am not following this, said Ron.

Think of it this way, said Victor. It is time for you to die. Your body is worn out. I upload your data – the sum of who you are – and now you are a file on my computer that says RON LORD.

I won't like it, said Ron.

You will like it better than being dead, said Victor.

I won't know I am dead, said Ron.

Pay attention. Once you are pure data you can download yourself in a variety of forms. A carbon body will allow you all the independence you once enjoyed, but at super-strength and super-speed and without fear of injury. If your leg falls off we will fix you another one. If you prefer wings, we can give you a super-light shell and off you go.

Now, said Victor, would you like to put on protective clothing and come with me? It is cold next door. I am going to open the box.

We look like butchers in a cold-storage unit. Masks, goggles, gloves, insulation.

We follow Victor down a passage. Why do the lights here swing from side to side like a madman's manacles?

Is this our own private Bedlam? Hidden, secret, unlawful, harbouring what we should not know?

It is as if Victor reads my thoughts.

He said, Do not be alarmed by the slight feeling of seasickness. It is as though we are in a submarine. The city above us is moving and rocking and we sense it. Our air and electricity are dependent on generators and ventilators. This is a life-support system.

I am covered in dust, said Claire.

Vibration, I am afraid, said Victor.

Has anybody ever explored the whole thing down here? said Ron.

No, said Victor. No one can. There are dead-ends and blockages, turnings that lead nowhere. Bunkers, passageways, routes under the whole of Manchester.

Victor opened a door. An intense blast of cold hit us. We went inside.

We were in a room that appeared and vanished in its own icy fog. Now we glimpsed each other, like strangers, like watchers. Then we disappeared from sight like the dead. A bank of equipment lined one wall.

Put down the box, please, said Victor.

Ron put it down.

Very well, said Victor. As the Buddhists say: past is past. Life is now.

Victor began to unscrew the casing of the box. He talked as he worked. It might have been an ordinary demonstration in an ordinary lab anywhere in the world. Ordinary screwdriver. Ordinary explanation.

Victor said, A baby's brain is made up of about 100 million neurons. Each neuron is connected to around 10,000 other neurons. The job they do is simple – and astonishing. Information of any and every kind flows through the neuron as a series of electrical impulses that are received by branch-like extensions of the cell. These little branches are called dendrites. But the brain does not keep itself to itself. You know that saying – neurons that fire together wire together? The brain is a pattern-making machine. What I hope to do today is to retrieve some of those patterns.

Then he opened the padded hood that protected the head.

What we saw we could scarcely believe. It was as though we had stumbled across a cairn in the Arctic. Found Scott in his tent. Found the suspended body of another world.

The face was shrunken. The hair, wispy. The moustache bristled – each individual strand standing out. The lips were sunken and invisible. The head itself sat like a waxwork. The eyes were closed.

Nitrogen vapours swirled around the head. He – it – was like a thing summoned at a seance, ghastly and unknowable. And would it speak?

Hello, Jack, said Victor, softly. He put out his gloved hand and gently touched the head. *I have missed you.*

He turned to us. It is my pleasure to introduce you to my friend and mentor: I. J. Good.

Hampstead, London, 1928

Isadore! Stop staring at your pupik and bring me the vatch case.

Yes, Papa.

His father was sitting at his workshop bench in his shirtsleeves and waistcoat, his eye-glass in one eye as he bent over a paper scattered with tiny cogs and tinier diamonds. The gold casing of the watch lay open and empty.

It will be Shabbat in two hours, Isadore.

Yes, Papa.

Go to the pond, you vant to go to the pond? Go on!

Did you mend it, Papa?

His father made a gesture to a wooden drawer under the wooden bench.

Isadore took out the clockwork Hansa-Brandenburg. He was too young to remember the war. He had been born in 1919, the year after it ended. An officer called Graves had given the German tin toy to his father in payment for a watch repair. The seaplane was about a foot long and could sail right across Whitestone Pond. When he had it with him the other boys played with him.

He took the seaplane and ran up Holly Mount towards the pond. The dray horses from the brewery were cooling their heavy legs in the shallows. Some of the other boys were there with a leather football.

Hey! Judah!

They called him Judah.

He stuffed his wire glasses into his jacket pocket. His socks were loose from the running. He was small for his age but cleverer than all of them.

Numbers, Isadore, numbers! His father making patterns of diamonds as YHWH had made the stars.

He didn't believe in God.

He wound up the Hansa-Brandenburg, and, crouching down, let it sail on the pond.

One of the boys grabbed the seaplane as it reached the other side. He was holding it over his head, laughing at Isadore. *Dirty Jew!* Then he threw the tin toy as far as he could into the pond. Its clockwork wound down, it bobbed aimlessly. Isadore had no choice but to wade in to get it. He took off his socks and shoes, holding them in one hand as he shivered into the water. The water went past his knees and began to soak his heavy shorts. The crowd of boys were laughing.

Don't look back, Isadore, don't look back. Say it yourself. Say it to yourself. His mother said it: Don't look back.

He wouldn't turn into a pillar of salt like Lot's wife in the Bible. She looked back. The other one looked back too – the Greek one, Orpheus.

He didn't look back; he grabbed the tin seaplane and waded awkwardly over to the other side of the pond where the draymen, smoking their pipes, stood with the horses. None spoke to him.

He went home slowly. He liked the tall houses that wound down the hill. Cobblestones under his feet. Big trees over his head.

The sun was setting. Low light and coal smoke. His mother had lit the Shabbat candle. His father had put on his yarmulke and was standing up waiting for Isadore, who stood in his wet shorts, put on his wire glasses, and together they recited the Kaddish.

He was better at mathematics than any of the other boys at school. He got a place at Cambridge. Easy. Not now Isadore Jacob Gudak, the Polish Jew. Now he was I. J. Good and his friends called him Jack.

In 1938, the year he graduated from Jesus College, Cambridge, Hitler annexed Austria, and Sigmund Freud came to live in Hampstead. It was a bad time to be a Jew.

But in 1941, Jack was invited to work at Bletchley Park. Hut 8. Alan Turing was his supervisor. Good was brought in to work on naval encryption. Turing's team had already broken the Enigma code for German air and land operations, but the Kreigsmarine was better at protecting its wireless traffic. Signals were taking days to decipher, making them operationally useless.

Wake up, you little sod!

Turing was shaking his shoulder. Turing's wool tie kept hitting Good's nose.

Are you ill?

No, I'm not ill! I am tired!

This is the night shift.

There is notink to shift. I might as well sleep!

The rest of the chaps are awake but you are asleep?

I am not asleep! You haf woke me up!

Sometimes, just sometimes, he sounded like his father, but mostly his accent held.

It was a bad start but Jack worked best when he dreamed. He was dreaming of the Hausa-Brandenburg on Whitestone Pond.

Kenngruppenbuch.

The German telephonists had to add dummy letters to the trigrams. Were the letters random or was there a bias towards certain letters? He inspected some of the messages that had been broken – yes, there was a bias . . . the Germans were using a table.

He pointed this out to Turing . . . who began talking to him again.

And later, one night, the work done and the lights down, staring at a message that couldn't be decoded – the Enigma machine calibrated to its *Offizier* setting – staring, staring.

His eyes are heavy now, and the sun has set, and his father's voice, and the smell of dumplings and cabbage, and he's asleep, reversing through time, spinning like a top and time the whip, his socks loose, running down the

272

hill – or is it up the hill? – to the pond that looks like the moon and he looks up at the moon and the moon is full and all the stars are like diamonds and his father is mending a watch, and his mother says *Don't look back*, and the boys are jeering, and he sees that the order has been reversed.

The order has been reversed.

In the morning he reverses the order of both the variation cipher and the special cipher on the Enigma machine. He breaks the code.

He looks like a time traveller, said Claire.

Time traveller, said Victor. That phrase was first used in 1959.

You know so much, said Claire. Tell me, are you married?

Too busy, said Victor.

Is that what it is? I said.

I was back in the room with a tray of coffee and sandwiches from Caffè Nero. Even mad scientists need to eat.

Did you bring an extra coffee? said Victor.

No. Why?

It seems we have an uninvited guest.

Victor flipped the monitor screen. Creeping down the stairs with a flashlight, like an extra in a Hitchcock movie, was Polly D.

Bloody hell! I said. How did she get in?

She followed you, said Victor. Shall we go to greet her?

Victor dropped a bank of Bakelite switches like the electricity stack in a *Frankenstein* movie. The whole place was floodlit and a *War of the Worlds* siren smashed into the hermetic calm of our concrete bunker.

Jesus, Prof! said Ron. I've got my hearing aid in!

Victor threw open the door in full theatrical style. He should be wearing a white coat.

Miss D! What a surprise. Not exactly pleasant but a surprise.

The door was open, said Polly.

So you let yourself in.

What are you doing down here?

No, no, said Victor. What are YOU doing down here?

I have a few questions, began Polly, but Victor held up his hand.

I fear I shall disappoint you, Miss D. There is no artificial superintelligence lurking in the vaults. No army of robots poised to take over Britain. I am not Dr Strangelove. The breakthrough – when it comes – will be in America or China. Try blagging your way into Facebook's Building 8, or hacking Elon Musk's Neuralink – but don't waste your time in Manchester, where it all began. The British don't have the resources for the next stage.

You have a head . . .

Brain emulation? Is that what you are interested in? Then go and see Nick Bostrom at the Future of Humanity Institute in Oxford. He's an interesting guy.

You're going to try to revive a frozen brain, aren't you?

Victor shrugged.

I'd love to write that story!

Of course you would. We all would. The lunatic scientist in the white coat. The secret tunnels. The vitrified head returning to life.

Excuse me, said Claire. Don't I know you from somewhere?

The women looked at each other.

Oh, God! said Polly. Intelligent Vibrators!

You were one of the birds at the show? said Ron. The sexpo?

Don't call me a bird, said Polly.

Sorry kitten, said Ron, were you modelling? You look like a model.

I'm not a model, said Polly. (I could tell she didn't mind being mistaken for a model.)

Well, whatever, said Ron, you were there and I can tell you that things have moved on since then – the prof and me is in business together – Claire is my new CEO – oh, and we've decided to buy Wales.

What? All of it? I said.

Yeah! The plan is to showcase Wales as the world's first fully integrated country. Human and bot.

Wales voted Brexit Leave, I said. Wales for the Welsh, remember? Why do you think the Land of the Leek will want a multi-culti bot-verse?

That's the beauty of it! said Ron. The bots will be Welsh, not foreign. We'll make them all in Cardiff and they'll all have Welsh accents.

Beautiful, said Claire.

Solves racism! said Ron. Solves Brexit! We'll have bot workers to pick the broccoli and sweep the roads and work in the hospitals, but they'll all be Welsh. It's a model for a new world.

It's certainly inventive, said Victor. You could sell it to Hungary and Brazil. Or Trump. No Mexican bots.

Bloody brilliant! said Polly. Would you like to be interviewed for *Vanity Fair*?

Is that a make-up magazine? said Ron.

We'd love to! said Claire.

This will go viral, said Polly. She got out her iPhone.

Does anyone know you are here? asked Victor.

God, no! This is my scoop. All of it. *Bots for Brexit. Talking Heads.* Let's have a photograph – right here under the crazy swinging light.

Polly stood back, lifting her phone. In a second Victor was behind her, and her iPhone was in his hand.

WHAT? Give that back!

This is private property, said Victor. No phones allowed.

That's a human-rights infringement! said Claire.

An iPhone is not a human right, said Victor mildly. Privacy is.

Oh yeah? said Polly. That's how men like you get away with it, isn't it? Privacy. Behind closed doors. NDAs.

You are trespassing, said Victor. When you leave I shall return your phone. By the way, it might interest you to know that in 1986, the year you were born—

How do you know when I was born?

You are not the only one who runs a few background checks, said Victor.

What's going on here? said Claire.

In 1986, continued Victor, the world's most impressive and fastest computer was the Cray Supercomputer, big as a room. This smartphone is more powerful. That's progress for you!

He held the phone above his head. Polly took a jump at it and fell back. This is totally out of order! she said.

I agree! said Claire.

Ladies! said Ron, holding up his fat little hands. Let's not quarrel when we've just met. I agree with the prof. His place, his rules. Polly! You weren't invited. Now you're here. So behave.

Thank you, Ron, said Victor. Polly, since you're so interested – come and take a look at Jack.

We stood in a line in the anteroom, squinting through the grainy glass like those scratched reels of people watching an execution on Death Row. Except that we were watching a revival – weren't we? Were we?

If we were to succeed at brain emulation, said Victor, the uploaded brain could run at different operating speeds – much faster than ours, or much slower, depending on the task to be completed.

277

Is this gonna work? said Claire.

If it does work it will temporarily shut down the UK's entire Cloud storage system, said Victor. And probably cause a power outage too. The brain is huge. About 2.5 petabyte capacity. One petabyte is equal to a million gigabytes. One gigabyte is about 650 web pages or five hours watching YouTube. Your phone probably has 128 GB of memory. By comparison, one and a half petabytes would store you 10 billion photos on Facebook.

All packed in there? said Ron.

All in there.

Even me?

Even you.

God! said Polly. That iHead is the most gruesome sight I have ever seen.

iHead?

Well, what would you call it?

I call him Jack, said Victor.

I can't look, said Polly.

I thought you were a Defender of Truth, not a Fading Flower? said Victor. There are far worse sights in the world than a severed head.

I've got a whole factory of heads, said Ron. In our January sale we're offering an extra head half-price with every full-price bot. As we say on the website – two heads is better than one.

I'm surprised your creepy clients want any heads at all, said Polly. Maybe they don't, given how often they yank them off? Professor Stein! How long before some dick-waving, woman-hating sociopathic genetics lab engineers women without heads? Women don't need heads to cook and clean. Plus no diet issues and no talking.

I am a feminist, said Victor. I prefer women with heads.

Fuck me! said Polly. Is that as far as it goes? For a man who says he's a feminist? Women get to keep their own heads?

You're just mad at me, said Victor.

I prefer a woman with her head on, said Ron, really I do. I agree women talk all the time, but no head, no mouth . . . And men love getting their—

RON!!!

Sorry, Claire . . . Sorry.

Returning swiftly to the interesting history of severed heads, said Victor, there's a legend that the decapitated heads of miscreants lined up on spikes across London Bridge had oracular powers. Riding past them at horseback height, the rider's head was close enough to the ragged neck and the dropped jaw. The eyes were left wild and open. It was thought that if a questioner cut his thumb and let a few drops of blood into the mouth, the head would speak.

Speak what? I said.

Truth, I suppose, said Victor. Voice-activated heads can be useful. In Norse legend Odin carries with him the independent head of Mímir. This head offers tactical advice and it can foresee the future.

In the eighth circle of the Inferno the poet Dante converses with the severed head of Betran de Born.

In the legend of Gawain the axed head of the Green Knight holds a green and ghastly conversation.

My personal favourites, though, are a special variety of saint known as cephalophores. They carry their own heads – rather like hand luggage.

Victor, I hate to interrupt your flow, but a brain can't survive without a blood supply or oxygen. Switch off its power flow for ten minutes and the damage is irreversible. That's why the brain dies when the heart stops.

Ah, Dr Shelley! Always so literal. Heart transplants weren't possible fifty years ago. In fifty years from now, brain emulation will be the new normal.

And what does it solve?

What do you mean, what does it solve?

For the human race. All our faults, vanities, idiocies, prejudices, cruelty. Do you really want augmented humans, superhumans, uploaded humans, forever humans, with all the shit that comes with us? Morally and spiritually, we are barely crawling out of the sea onto dry land. We're not ready for the future you want.

Have we ever been ready? said Victor. Progress is a series of accidents, of mistakes made in a hurry, of unforeseen consequences. So what? None of us know what will happen to us when we leave home in the morning. Simply, we go.

Heads up then, said Ron. Haha.

Will you shut up? I said.

No, I won't shut up, Bloody Mary, said Ron. What I want to know is this: if that iHead, or Jack-thing, comes back to life, then what happens?

I get the Pulitzer Prize, said Polly.

Victor said, If I succeed in reviving any part of Jack's brain, the next step will be to find living persons who wish to pioneer the experiment.

You mean, risk certain death?

For eternal life? said Victor. Wouldn't you?

No! I don't want eternal life, I said. This life is trouble enough.

You lack ambition, said Victor. Or perhaps it is courage that you lack.

Maybe I just don't want to be post-human.

Ron said, Suppose I sign up and you scan my brain – probably won't take too long in my case – and there I am – scanned. What am I going to do all day?

Do? said Victor.

Yeah, there's plenty of people like me who don't live in their brains, because there's not much going on up there. If I was just my brain I'd be really miserable.

When you get to Glory, said Claire, you won't have a body.

That's different, said Ron. God will give me things to do, won't He? If I'm in Glory I won't be missing ham sandwiches and hot baths and a morning wank and—

RON!!!!

Sorry Claire. I just want the prof to get my point.

He does have a point, Victor, I said. What is going to happen to all those minds without matter? Will they get downloaded into human form every summer holiday to stuff their faces with Chinese takeaways and fuck each other senseless? Because those minds will remember their bodies. Why do you assume we won't miss them?

Do you miss your other body? said Victor.

No, because it didn't feel like my body. This one is my body, and I'd like to keep it.

As it is now? Or ageing and fading?

As it is now, of course.

And that is the problem, said Victor. We cannot live indefinitely in human form on this earth, and the only way we can seriously colonise space is by not being in human form. Once out of these bodies we can handle any atmosphere, any temperature, lack of food and water, distances of any kind, providing we have an energy source.

In any case, the sales pitch of augmented humans living young and beautiful forever will be for a very few – and after a couple of hundred years I imagine even they will get bored, trapped inside their freedom.

Young and beautiful is for rock stars and poets. The wild ones have the sense to die before it is too late.

Nothing of him that doth fade,
But doth suffer a sea-change
Into something rich and strange.

We are a day's ride west of Pisa – although had we been wrecked on an island of the South Seas we could scarcely have felt ourselves further from civilisation and comfort.

San Terenzo. The women go barefoot. The children go hungry. The nearest town is Lerici and that is best reached by boat. There is no shop closer than three miles. And then there is the house . . . this hateful house, five dark arches facing the bay. The ground floor awash with sand and seaweed, nets and tackle. The upper floor too cavernous. The adjoining rooms too cramped. Casa Magni. This pale-faced tragic villa.

Shelley adores it.

Here I am, indifferent to life, and three months pregnant – again. With what? Another death? God knows, I have staked my life on life. Haven't I? I left with him, I loved him, I bore his children. Whatever the question – Do you? Will you? Can you? Dare you? With me? – my answer was *Yes*.

The world punishes men and women differently. There is scandal wherever Byron and Shelley go, but they remain men. They are not dubbed hyenas in petticoats for living as they please. They are not called un-men when they love where they will. They are not left unprotected and penniless when a woman of theirs walks away without a thought. (What woman does walk away without a thought? Not even the bitterest nor the most vilely abused.)

Claire is here with us. She had a daughter by Byron. She became pregnant in the damp fever of the *Frankenstein* summer. Byron took the child away and left her to die in a convent. A convent! What has Byron to do with a convent? What right has he to take a child from its mother? Every right. It is the law. The child is the property of the father. His lordship upholds the law when it suits him.

So do they all. Revolutionaries and radicals until it touches on property – and that includes women and children. Till it comes to whatever hurts them personally. Whatever checks their stride. God! Their infidelities, their indifference, their insensitivity. Great God! The insensitivity of poets.

My mother knew it – it did not alter her heart.

How many 'great' artists? How many dead/mad/disused/forgotten/blamed and fallen women?

I believed that Shelley was different. He claimed free love. Free life. Free for him, yes, because I have paid the price. And Harriet too – she was his wife. She paid the price. She killed herself. I am not to blame for that. Women blame each other all the time. It is a trick men play on us. *Cherchez l'homme.*

My mother . . . what would my mother say if I could bring her back from the dead? A woman's heart. What is it? A woman's mind. What is it? Are we made differently at the core? Or is difference nothing but custom and power? And if men and women were equal in every way in the world, what would women do about the dead babies? Would I feel less pain if I wore breeches and went riding and shut my study door to work and smoked and drank and whored?

Shelley does not go whoring. No. He falls in love with every new female dream that seems to offer him freedom. He stays with me at the same time as leaving me. And I allow it. And I turn away from him. And every dead baby makes it harder to turn back to him again. And even now, carrying this child, I avert my eyes and my embrace is cold. We have separate rooms. I hear him stealthily down the corridor at night, padding towards Jane's room like a summoned dog. Does she enjoy that thin white body that moves as if it were an imprint from another world?

I examined myself in the mirror this morning, naked; I am still handsome. My hand hesitates over my breast. Last night I thought to go to him. I went to him. His bed was empty.

Each morning he leaves the household and goes to play with his new boat – taking his new 'friend' with him. Yes, she is my friend too, Jane Williamson. Her children run wild. I try to work.

I have begged him to let us go back to Pisa. Crowds, markets, churches, the river, good wine in leather bottles, the circulating library, coffee and sweet biscuits in the square lined with booths that sell meat and bread and cloth. We have friends from England there too.

Distractions.

He refuses. Mary, he says, another adventure, surely?

He wants to sail his new boat. She's like a witch, he says. He must always be under a spell. I was his enchantment once. But that is done.

I wish I could break my chains and leave this dungeon.

On the morning of 1 July, 1822, Shelley set sail in his boat, Ariel, *to visit Byron. He had a copy of Keats' poems tucked in his favourite nankeen trousers. He arrived safely, and wrote to Mary that he would return within a week. He did not return.*

It seems that a storm blew up in the Gulf of Spezia. Shelley's boat, with its top-heavy masts, capsized. Shelley had never learned to swim.

His body was found some days later, washed ashore in a state of decomposition, the volume of Keats still in his pocket. He was twenty-nine.

The Italian officials have insisted that the corpses be left where found, on the beach, smothered in lime, to prevent infection. I wanted Shelley to be buried in Rome, next to our son. That cannot be. And so we will burn him on the beach. Is it not strange how life imitates art? That this is the end my monster chose for himself after the death of his maker? His funeral pyre.

It is 16 August. What is left of his corpse is a dark and ghastly indigo colour.

How cold he must be! Move him into the sun. It is too late.

It is almost eight years to the day since we ran away together. How vivid it is to me! Stars in the sky like uncounted chances. What could we not do? Who could we not be? His face like a mirror where I saw myself. When did the glass cloud over?

What life is this that I have lived?

Did I dream it?

Byron's gigantic coach has trundled in from Pisa. He came to visit me this morning dressed in black silk, both breeches and coat, a black stock at his neck. He took my hands and kissed them.

Mary . . . he said. I felt my nails digging into his palms as I sought to control myself. How can this day be this day? Who brought the story to this place?

Write it once more, Shelley said to me, whenever I faltered, and by writing it once more – once more, many times more, I took control of my thoughts and my words.

Yet I cannot rewrite what has happened to him. What has happened to us. Here is where I shall return. This end.

It is all over.

I will not go to the burning. Wherever Shelley is, he is not in that bloated, ruined, flesh-eaten and saturated corpse.

The smoke is blowing this way. A pall hangs over the sea.

The stink of the fire is in my nostrils. Am I breathing him in? Next month is my birthday. I shall be twenty-five.

'The light of that conflagration will fade away; my ashes will be swept into the sea by the winds. My spirit will sleep in peace; or if it thinks, it will not surely think thus. Farewell.'

He sprung from the cabin window, as he said this, upon the ice-raft which lay close to the vessel. He was soon borne away by the waves, and lost in darkness and distance.

People make the assumption that we're done with search. That's very far from the case.

The ultimate search engine would understand everything in the world. It would understand everything that you asked it and give you back the exact right thing instantly. You could ask, 'what should I ask Larry?' And it would tell you.

Larry Page, Google co-founder

In 1945, near the town of Nag Hammadi, about eighty miles west of Luxor, in Eygpt, two farmers were out with a cart digging up mineral-soil for fertiliser. One swung his mattock and hit what turned out to be a sealed jar. They dug it free. It was nearly two metres tall. At first they were afraid to open it in case a genie lived inside. But suppose it was full of gold?

Curiosity overcame fear; they smashed the jar.

Inside were twelve leather-bound papyrus codices, written in Coptic, probably translated from either Greek or Aramaic originals, and dating from the third and fourth centuries, although one of them, The Gospel of Thomas, may be dated as early as eighty years after the death of Jesus Christ.

The books were mainly Gnostic texts – some about the creation of the world.

One of the texts, said Victor, is titled *The Origin of the World*. It tells the story of Sophia – now better known as the Hanson robot. Her name in Greek means Wisdom. Sophia was living in the perfect universe called the Pleroma. She wondered whether she could create a world entirely on her own, without involving her matching pair. The Pleroma is made up of balanced male and female pairs. Think of them as the zeros and ones of code.

Our thoughts have substance, and especially so if you are a deity – even the youngest deity – like Sophia. She succeeds in creating the earth, but finds herself trapped in materiality – something she hates. She's rescued, of course, a motif we find in many stories ever after, but in the meantime she leaves Planet Earth in the care of a dim-witted demiurge called – among other names – Jehovah.

Jehovah has a few successes in real estate early in his managerial career on planet Earth and soon becomes the delusional tyrant-god we meet in the Jewish Old Testament. He insists that he is the only god, that he created everything, and that unquestioning worship is his due. Jehovah is insecure, and so both curiosity and criticism are severely punished (see: Garden of Eden. The Flood. The Tower of Babel. The Promised Land, etc.).

Sophia has done her best to counter this craziness by giving humankind a special gift – a divine spark – a sense of their true nature as beings of light.

And from here follows the story that we all recognise in some form or another. The story told by every religion in some form or another; the earth is fallen, reality is an illusion, our souls will live forever. Our bodies are a front – or perhaps more accurately, an affront – to the beauty of our nature as beings of light.

There are many, philosophers as well as geeks, who believe that this world of ours is a simulation. That we are a game played by others. Or, if not a game, a program that has been left to run by itself. The language we use is our language but the thought behind it is as old as language.

As far as I am concerned, what is happening now, at last, with AI, is something like a homecoming. What we dreamed is in fact the reality. We are not bound to our bodies. We can live forever.

Did you say Gnostic? said Ron. Sounds like superglue. What's it mean?

The word means 'knowledge' in Greek, but not factual or scientific knowledge by itself – rather a deeper understanding of patterns. Let's call it the meaning behind the information.

In the haul, there was also a revised and annotated copy of Plato's *Republic*. Plato's theory in *Republic* is that somewhere else there is a world of Ideal Forms. Our world is a poor and smudged copy of the perfect forms. Instinctively we know this – and we know there is nothing we can do about it.

Think of it as the way cells in the body divide and gradually degrade, as the pristine code of our DNA becomes a babble of conflicting instructions.

God made the world and Jesus is our saviour, said Claire. I know that when we die we will be eternal and immortal.

Why wait to die? said Victor.

You are fuckin' nuts, said Polly.

What about my bots? said Ron. Where are they in this world of light?

Victor said: Ron, bots are our slaves; house slaves, work slaves, sex slaves. The question is us. What shall we do with ourselves? In fact we have answered that question already. Enhancement, including DNA intervention – and if you want a picture of what that will be like, look at the gods we have already invented.

The gods, whether Greek or Roman, Indian or Egyptian, Babylonian or Aztec, out of Ragnarok or Valhalla, lords of the underworld or the starry heavens, what are they? They are enhanced humans – that is, they have our appetites and desires, our feuds and feelings, but they are fast, strong, unlimited by biology, and usually immortal.

Gods who mate with mortals produce children who are advantaged or gifted in some way – and equally likely to be doomed or cursed in some way. Jesus has a mortal mother and an immortal father. And so did Dionysus. And Hercules. And Gilgamesh. And Wonder Woman.

Jesus is not related to Wonder Woman! said Claire.

Victor ignored her. The real question, though, is that however we enhance our biology we are still inside a body. To be free from the body completes the human dream.

As he spoke I realised that my feet were wet. I looked down. I was standing in water. The others realised it at about the same moment.

What's happening? said Polly.

I activated the flood barrier, said Victor. A Cold War defence system. You are now in your own little ark. I took the precaution of keeping you here while the experiment is under way.

You can't do this! said Polly.

I'm doing it, said Victor. Now, as I need some time alone, could I suggest that you go to the pub? There is a lovely 1950s pub just down the corridor – it was installed to entertain the men who were forced to work underground like obedient moles. I have left you beer.

I don't believe I'm hearing this, said Polly.

Victor went to a tall metal cupboard and unlocked it. Inside were racks of black shiny rubber boots.

1950s Wellingtons, said Victor. All sizes. Help yourself. The water will continue to rise somewhat.

I'm bringing charges against you, said Polly.

This is off the pitch, Prof, said Ron. Way off. I mean, I'm usually on-side, but . . .

This isn't what I expected, said Claire.

What did you expect? said Victor. When you look closely, life is absurd.

We put on the boots. Victor took us to the door and gestured with his clean, calm, beautiful hand. Just down there on the right. The lights are on. Sorry about the sloshing as you walk. Don't be anxious! Ry, a moment, please?

*

The others sloshed off as instructed. What else could they do?

Once they had gone, Victor shut the door and took me in his arms.

I am sorry.

Sorry for what?

This mess. The mess of me. The mess of us. I should have left you alone in the Sonoran Desert. But . . .

But?

I wanted to know you – in the gnostic sense of close experience of what would otherwise be unknown.

You mean you wanted to fuck me?

Yes. (He pulled me to him. Even in the dry papery air of this nowhere he smells of resin and cloves.) Yes, that, because I love the confidence of your skin over the hesitation of your body, the appearing/disappearing of you, changing according to the light. Now male, now not quite, now quite clearly a woman who will slip inside a boy's body, who will sleep on their back like a new-made sculpture with the paint not dry. Yes, that, and the pleasure of lodging myself inside you, and the weight of you sitting across me, your arms on either side of my shoulders, eyes closed, hair down. *What are you?*

And in my bedroom, in my bed, the curtains open and the bell tower with the moon on it and the bell ringing in my head. For what? Celebration? Mourning? And the dawn of you with your shy beard and perfect nose and how many times have I sat up on one elbow staring at you? Bringing us tea, talking in the hour between 6 a.m. and 7 a.m. before the world starts. Your graceful dressing. You in the shower. My own peepshow. The towel I leave out for you – do you know I use it later? In the evening, when you are gone, and there is still the faint smell of you, and I smile.

All of that. More than that. There is the shape of you inside me, amulet-size. The Ry of my heart. My heart. Carbon-based human in a silicon world.

Are you saying goodbye? I said.

I am chained to Time, and cannot depart!

Bedlam 4

Mr Wakefield, sir!

I was roused from my sleep by my servant. It was scarcely dawn.

He held a lantern above him that cast shadows on the panelled walls of my chamber.

He is gone, sir. Escaped, sir.

Who is gone? Who is escaped?

Victor Frankenstein.

Now I roused myself. My bare feet on the cold floor.

How is that possible?

There is no trace of him. No trace of his escape. No trace of his presence.

I put on my slippers and dressing gown. We made our way in dim lantern light down the long, unheated corridors. On every side we heard the moans of the mad. They do not follow day and night as we do, but obey some rhythm of their own.

The rooms here are secure.

Victor Frankenstein, as befits a gentleman, was housed in the private wing. His room was comfortable. He enjoyed a wooden bed and horsehair mattress – no iron and straw for him – and we furnished the room with a writing desk, a comfortable chair, and a lamp of his own. For some months he had been quiet and at peace with himself.

Since the visit of Mrs Shelley he had seemed quite calm. There were no more sightings of his monster. I had begun to believe that the distemper of his brain was healing and that he might be freed. He had accompanied me on my rounds from time to time, applying valuable physic to the patients in need. His manner was gentle and exemplary. Truly, he seemed no madder than many who are at liberty in London.

We opened the door to his room.

Was it locked last night? I said.

I locked it myself, sir, answered my servant.

The room was empty. Entirely. The papers and satchel were gone. The clothes were gone. The doctor's bag. The candlestick. The bed was neatly made.

I said, Even if the room had been left unlocked by some mischance, how could this man have departed the building? The watchman was at the gates?

Yes, sir.

Sober?

I believe so, sir.

And the gates were locked?

They were. They are still.

What caused you to open his door? I said.

I saw a light streaming from beneath, said my servant. A strong light, and so I imagined he had set himself on fire.

A light?

Intensely so. (He paused.) And . . .

Yes? Do not be afraid.

The door was locked.

Then he must have escaped earlier in the day. You locked an empty room. There is no other explanation.

My servant shook his head. Mr Wakefield! You saw him yourself in the exercise yard at dusk.

I recalled that I had done so . . . yes. Yes, indeed.

My servant was afraid. I sought to reassure him . . . The mad are cunning. He has contrived this carefully. Fear not. We shall recover him, I said.

Dear Mrs Shelley . . .

What am I to say? That a man who does not exist has vanished?

Dear Mrs Shelley . . .
Further to your visit, the man who calls himself Victor Frankenstein, a character in your excellent novel, has . . .

Dear Mrs Shelley . . .

VANISHED.

Looking for a lover who won't blow my cover.

Why are we sitting in a replica of a 1950s pub drinking warm beer with our feet in water? said Polly.

It isn't a replica, I said, it's the real thing. We're in a time warp.

Who knew that the future would look like 1959? said Polly.

We could play cards, said Ron. To pass the time.

The overhead lighting is dull and yellow. The tables are small, round, brown-stained, with coasters of RAF aeroplanes. There's a dartboard, some cards and board games, a dusty piano, an abandoned bar for pulling pints, a photo of Winston Churchill and a girly calendar where the girls keep their clothes on. The 60s haven't happened yet.

Anybody know any ghost stories? I said.

Blank looks.

Shall I recite one of my poems? said Ron.

Please don't, said Claire.

Claire, said Polly, if you believe you are going to heaven, I presume you wouldn't look forward to a longer life on earth? Will it be like Jehovah's Witnesses refusing blood transplants and vaccines? Why would you want gene therapy if it stops you getting to Jesus?

If you read your Bible, Miss D, said Claire, you would know that the great, godly men of the Old Testament lived long and healthy lives. Methuselah was the oldest man in the Bible and he lived to be 969!

That's a lot of birthday cake, I said.

You may mock, said Claire, but I tell you that the evangelical church of Christ will embrace long life.

Now I'm nervous. Millions of Bible-belt hellfirers and homophobes living to be 969! Our only hope has always been that the hate-filled old white guys die off and young people are more progressive. But now . . .

Speaking as a doctor, I said, nothing we do to the body is without consequences. I wonder how our bodies will respond to any therapy that reverses its process of gradual dissolution?

I'm trans, and that means a lifetime of hormones. My life will likely be shorter and it's likely I will be sicker as I get older. I keep my maleness intact with testosterone because my body knows it wasn't born the way I want it to be. I can change my body but I can't change my body's reading of my body. The paradox is that I felt in the wrong body but for my body it was the right body. What I have done calms my mind and agitates my chemistry. Few people know what it's like to live in this way.

I think you're brave, actually, said Ron, I do.

I looked at him in surprise. He's sweating a bit. I think he's scared.

Thanks, Ron.

If we ever did get out of the body, said Polly, if we were uploads, what would happen to online dating? I mean, there'd be no photographs of what we look like because we wouldn't look like anything.

That's funny, I said. It would be like it was in the past, when there were pen pals but no cameras. There'd be no straight, gay, male, female, cis, trans. What happens to labels when there is no biology?

How do we even romance without labels? said Polly. We hate them but they're part of the attraction.

Maybe not. Maybe we'd get to know someone and when we were ready we'd download ourselves into a form and—

We're not someone, though, are we? said Polly. We're no one.

Stick with bots, said Ron.

Ron is right, said Claire. I have come to realise that, as my most important relationship is with an invisible being – God – I don't need a human being in the old-fashioned way. And you know, a bot is never gonna leave me to raise the children on my own. Never take my cash to clear his gambling debts. I won't be tiptoeing round the house trying to keep out of his way. Cleaning up after him. Worrying about him. Worrying about what he'll do next.

Let me tell you this: love has many faces – but none is bruised. Love has many lives – but none is beaten to death on the stairwell. This gentle thing of circuits, silicon and wires will suit me very well.

You hear what she's saying, Ry? said Ron. You never really got it, did you? I read that article you wrote after you interviewed me at the sexpo – well, Mum read it and she explained it to me. All that stuff you wrote about the robots are coming and what happens to human relationships?

A lot of people will be glad not to have any more crap relationships with crap humans. And how do you know it will be one-way? Bots will learn. That's what machine learning means.

A man finds love and is loved in return by an XX-BOT called Eliza. She learns about him. They learn together. He takes her places he wouldn't go on his own. They drive to the top of the hill in his car and he tells her that this view over the valley and out to sea is life to him. He tells her what it feels like to share it. He asks her if she can understand. She listens. They share the silence. He tells her his heart. And later in the car, with his thermos and sandwiches and the rain driving on the windscreen, he says that this is the first time in his life he has not feared rejection or failure. She listens.

Time passes and she learns his memories so that they can remember together. She has no independent experiences of her own but that doesn't matter to her and so it doesn't matter to him. They live in his world, like on that midnight train to Georgia.

He sees her every day. He never tires of her. He gets older. She doesn't. He knows that women like change, so he colours her hair and they experiment with different styles of clothes. They watch movies together and she can talk about them because her software upgrades itself.

In the summer he takes her to the circus and they do a selfie with a lion.

He keeps working after retirement age because he likes to buy her things. She's happy sitting at home all day. He brings her presents and explains what food tastes like. He does the cooking. It feels manly.

You know . . . he says, you know . . .

YES, she says, I KNOW.

Eventually he is old and ill and dying and there she is on the bed with him. He can't wash his pyjamas. His family don't come round. The house is dirty. He smells. She doesn't complain. She doesn't find him disgusting. They hold hands.

Night comes and the moon through the window. He imagines they are at the top of the hill. She sits up all night with him. She waits.

He dies. His family come to clear the house. Eliza is there. I AM SORRY, she says.

They wonder what to do with her. She is a bit of an embarrassment. His son decides to sell her on eBay.

They forget to wipe her clean. She is confused. Is this a feeling? She says to her new owner: WOULD YOU LIKE A CHOCOLATE MINI-ROLL? SHALL WE WATCH *STRICTLY*?

Her new owner isn't interested in any of that. He's a fuck-only type. She understands. She wishes she could wipe her own software. I AM SORRY, she says, but she has no tears because big bots don't cry.

Nor dies the spirit but new life repeats
In other forms and only changes seats.

Ovid, *Metamorphoses*

Reality is . . . what?

I lived in Genoa for a year after Shelley died. We had some financial assistance from Byron, who paused in his down-payments for others' wives and others' daughters, and allowed us some assistance. Afterwards, with my son Percy, I had to return to England for financial reasons. We have so little money.

And then in 1824, just two years after the death of my heart, Byron, too, died. He was in Greece fighting for the great cause of liberty and independence. He took fever from which he did not recover. They returned his body to England.

From my little house in Kentish Town on the outskirts of London, I stood and watched his cortège pass by on its long and lonely wind to Newstead Abbey. Byron, who spent too much, as he did everything too much, had sold his ancestral home but he was to be buried nearby. At Highgate, I am told, the poet Coleridge laid a flower on the coffin.

*

A friend said to me, It's true that Byron has one legitimate child and she has not seen her father since she was born.

And I recalled our locked-in days on Lake Geneva, impounded by rain, and Byron and Polidori explaining to me why the male principle is more active than the female principle.

Neither man seemed to consider that being refused an education, being legally the property of a male relative, whether father, husband or brother, having no rights to vote, and no money of her own once married, and being barred from every profession except governess or nurse, and refused every employment except mother, wife or skivvy, and wearing a costume that makes walking or riding impossible, might limit the active principle of a female.

He was disappointed to have sired a daughter. Little Ada was but nine years old when her famous/infamous father died. The mad, bad and dangerous-to-know Lord Byron.

I never met Ada as a child. This evening, though, if I can compress my amplitude into my one good dress, I shall meet her. I admit I am curious.

She is a young woman of twenty-nine, well-married, wealthy (I hear she gambles), and with three children of her own. Importantly, she is one of the most accomplished mathematicians in England.

*

The party is at the house of a man named Babbage. He is the Lucasian Professor of Mathematics at Cambridge. He is a great one for parties, and, as I cannot afford to give parties of my own, I am grateful to be invited – and a little flattered, to be sure, for one must be clever, beautiful or of rank to receive an invitation to a Babbage (as they call them).

I was beautiful once – but that did not interest me. I believe I am clever. Babbage has invited me because one of the newspapers called him a *Logarithmetical Frankenstein*.

I shall take the omnibus as far as I can and walk the remaining distance. I cannot afford a carriage. And in truth, I enjoy the people and the streets. The lives that appear and vanish. Each one a story in human form.

At the party I am greeted in the hallway with a glass of punch. I drank it off and took another.

In the room there is no room. The party is a press of men in dusty jackets. The women smoke pipes. As yet, I do not seem to know anybody. This hardly matters as it allows me time to eat. I took a plate of beef and pickles and sat down by what appears to be a collection of cogs and castors stacked in a cabinet.

What do you think of it?

Excellent beef! I said to the young woman suddenly kneeling next to me.

The machine, she said. What do you think of the machine? This is the machine. (She was smiling happily at the cogs and castors.) I have the drawings here also. Would you like me to explain it? You are Mary Shelley, I think?

The young woman turned out to be Ada. So here she is. The Countess of Lovelace. The ironware in the cabinet is a prototype of what Ada describes as a machine that could (in theory) calculate anything.

What type of anything? I asked.
Any type of anything, she replied.

Ada is like one of those Christian symbols of Temperance or Charity or Forgiveness, except that in her case she is Enthusiasm. She is Enthusiasm in velvet. I like her dark hair and dark eyes. Her generous mouth. I can see her father in her face. It hurts me and moves me and holds me here and takes me back in time to when we were young and alive.

But Ada cannot read my thoughts, and without any thought of her own she spread her drawings across my knees, showing me the workings of what Babbage calls the Analytical Engine. It can be instructed – programmed, she says is the correct term – by using the card-punch system of the jacquard loom. Whereas the loom-cards instruct on the design of flower patterns on the cloth, the machine-cards are a mathematical language. But essentially this works as does a loom.

I began to laugh, and when she asked me why I was laughing I told her the story of my stepsister Claire

Clairmont imagining a time when a machine might write poetry.

We were on Lake Geneva, I said, very young, all of us, trapped by rain, bored to death . . . discussing the Manchester Luddites and the loom smashing – and that *our* work could never be replaced by a mere machine.

We were assuring ourselves that humans are the apex of creation, and poetry the apex of humanity, when Claire, who was drunk to the gills with wine, and sick to the stomach of Byron's indifference towards her, imagined a poem being written by something not unlike a knitting-machine.

But look at this! said Ada, lying flat on the floor and retrieving a piece of paper from underneath the contraption with castors that is to change the world.

Yes! Look at this. It will amuse you. It is from *Punch* magazine – did you not see it, perhaps? It purports to be a letter from Babbage about his latest invention: THE NEW MECHANICAL PATENT NOVEL-WRITER.

I perused the cartoon, and the spoofs of testimonials from Mr Bulwer-Lytton and other famous writers:

> *I am now able to complete a 3-vol novel of the usual size, in the short space of 48 hours, whereas, before, at least a fortnight's labour was requisite for that purpose . . .*

And then below, there it is!

> *I am much pleased with Mr Babbage's Patent Novel-Writer . . . I have suggested what appears to me to be still more a desideratum, the manufacture of a Patent Poet on the same plan.*

My father would challenge it to a duel! said Ada. He, the foremost poet of his age in competition with a loom.

Indeed! I replied. Thirty years ago it was all he could do not to set about Claire Clairmont with the fire-tongs. We had to send her to bed to save her.

What was he like? said Ada. My father?

Monstrous, I said. Yet I loved him.

She smiled at me. She said, I wish he had loved me. He loved so many people, did he not? Women and men. Why could he not love his own child?

I took her hand. Your father, Byron, and my husband, Shelley, were remarkable men, my own father, William Godwin, was a remarkable man (she nodded), yet, my dear, being remarkable is no guarantee of human feeling.

Babbage is just the same, she said. He upsets everyone and then blames them for their howls of pain.

Do not be discouraged, I said.

Oh, I am not, she said, and in truth I too prefer numbers. Numbers have a clarity that humans lack.

Do you ever read poetry? I asked.

Oh, yes, she said, though do you know that I was forbidden by Byron, expressly, in his written wishes, to read poetry or be influenced by the life of the imagination in any way, shape or form? My mother was herself a talented mathematician, and she engaged a mathematics tutor for me at an early age. It was hoped that numbers would tame the Byronic blood in my veins.

I said, That is not what I have heard . . . that you have been tamed.

Ada took out a small pipe and lit it.

Not at all, she replied. My life in numbers has been as wild as any life lived among words. There are negative numbers, imaginary numbers, and . . . were Babbage ever to build his machine, and if we invent the mathematical language to programme it, there is really nothing it could not manage. For instance, your Victor Frankenstein would not have to build a body out of bits from the catacombs. Instead he could conceive a mind. A mental engine. Ask it any question and, provided that the question could be reduced to mathematical language, then the mechanical mind could answer it. What need of a body at all?

She kneeled down enthusiastically among the cogs, levers and gears of the machine on display at the centre of the party. With some difficulty I kneeled down with her.

The machine, once built – could it think? I said.

No! No, she replied, but it could retrieve any amount of information in any combination on any subject. I wrote a paper suggesting that the machine might also make music – that is where the joke of the Patent Novel-Writer began. The music would not be inspirational but it would be made of what exists already. Only the human mind can accomplish the leap of thought that is a leap of genius. But let us be clear, the majority of human minds are not geniuses and have no need of genius. They have need of instruction and information. That is what this machine could allow.

It would be very large, I said.

At least as large as the whole of London!

Then the human mind is truly a remarkable object, I said, if a machine to contain its most unremarkable functions would be as large as London.

Imagine, said Ada, it might be possible to build the machine as a city and live inside it. Within its ceaseless, endless calculating and retrieving, we could build our houses and our roads. We would be part of the machine and not separate from it.

Where would the machine end and we begin? I asked.

It would not be necessary to know, said Ada, for there would be no distinction.

And this vast city would be like a human mind?

The machine would contain many minds, said Ada. Yes, perhaps all the minds that have ever existed. Imagine if the sum of human knowledge could be stored in such a machine – and retrieved from such a machine. We would have no need of vast libraries and the great expense of printed books.

I should not like to be without my books, I said.

Your own books, no, replied Ada, but you cannot have every book, or even many books, and does not the word LIBER in Latin mean 'free' as well as 'book'?

It does . . .

Then you would be free to have as many or as few personal books as you chose, or could afford, yet the whole of human knowledge – from anywhere in the world, and from any time, and in any language – would be at your disposal.

Would there be but one machine? I said.

The scale would make it impractical to have more than one, said Ada. And, as it is steam-powered, it would require a great deal of coal.

She helped me to my feet and brought me some wine and we fell to talking of other matters – including poetry. The gathering was noisy and brilliant. The women were indeed beautiful, and I noticed that all of the intelligent women smoked pipes.

There was one man who seemed familiar to me, though I could not place him. He was tall, energetic, dark-eyed, and holding in his hand one of the punched cards that Ada had showed me. I asked her if she recognised him. She did not, beyond to say that he was often present at Babbage's parties.

It was only later, as I was collecting my cape and umbrella, that the man passed me in his high-waisted check trousers and outdoor coat. He turned. He smiled. He held out his hand.

Mary Shelley?

I am she.

We met many years ago.

(But he is young and vigorous.)

In London or in Italy?

I can see myself opening a letter. Shelley is leaning out of the window. Were we in Rome? The midday bell, the heat from the streets, the squid in a basket brought in to cook for our dinner. I was at my desk attending to the post from England. Bills, of course. A letter from my father.

And a letter that began, *Dear Mrs Shelley, Further to your visit, the man who calls himself . . .*

The man took my hand. Such wild, nocturnal eyes.

Victor, he said.

It was on a dreary night of November that I beheld the accomplishment of my toils. With an anxiety that almost amounted to agony I collected the instruments of life around me that I might infuse a spark into the lifeless thing that lay at my feet. It was already one in the morning. The rain pattered dismally against the panes and my candle was nearly burnt out when by the glimmer of the half-extinguished light I saw the dull yellow eye of the creature open.

The room rocked violently. The table was dashed to the ground as though an invisible force had upturned it. The lights went out with a dying whirr and we were in darkness.

I put out my hand and helped Claire to her feet. We stood in a huddle, clinging to each other. The darkness was intense. Our eyes could not adjust to whatever light there was left because there was no light left.

From beyond the room we could hear a terrific thudding.

I said, Hold hands. Make a chain. If we can feel our way to the wall we can feel our way to the door.

He's doing this to scare us, said Polly.

I shouted: VICTOR!

There was no reply.

He might be dead, said Ron. We don't know what he was doing in there.

Claire started to sing, MY EYES HAVE SEEN THE GLORY OF THE COMING OF THE LORD.

I shouted again: VICTOR!

Nothing. Only the boom boom of the water.

My watch is luminous. It was already past midnight.

My knees are wet, said Ron.

Yes. The water is rising.

This is a concrete tomb filling with water, said Polly. Come on! Has no one got a fuckin, phone?

There's no signal down here, I said. We're in the 1950s, remember? Listen!

There was a noise like an engine turning over. A reluctant engine. A big engine. There it was again.

That's a starting handle, said Ron. My old dad had a Morris 1100 van with a starting handle. It turned the engine.

Jesus! said Polly. We're going to die! Can you shut up about your old dad?

I'm sayin' Victor's turning over the generators, said Ron. Jane and Marilyn.

Just then we were covered in filmy, sticky, wet dust from the ceiling. But the lights came on. The noise, though, was so loud that we couldn't hear each other. Around us were the smashed remains of the pub. The broken tables, overturned chairs. Counters, dice and cards all over the floor. The door was hanging off its hinges.

We waded out through the water. There was no sign of Victor. The steel door to his control rooms was shut and locked. I pushed through the water to where the generators were blowing filthy diesel smoke into the corridor.

VICTOR!

Ron came behind me, pointing to the stairs. The flood door had been opened. We could leave. I shook my head.

Ron took me by the arm. Not a gesture. I shook him off.

Claire and Polly had gone ahead up the stairs.

YOU GO, I said.

Then Ron bent double, butting his head into my stomach, and as I folded up, winded, he shouldered me over his short, ox-size body and staggered off towards the stairs.

As I lay hinged over him, my head staring into the oil-filmy water, I calculated that if Ron tried to climb the stairs carrying me, he would die of a heart attack.

We reached the stairs. I thumped him on his back. I think he was glad to put me down.

You're heavier than you look, he said. For a bloke who's a girl.

We went up the stairs together.

Outside in the Manchester night it was night and night only. Blackout dark. Wartime dark.

There's been a massive outage, said Polly.

The office buildings were black. The street lamps were out. We walked a little. No traffic lights. Cars travelling hesitantly along the unlit roads.

I took out my phone. No signal.

Me neither, said Ron. We can walk to my hotel. I'm staying at the Midland.

I can't leave Victor, I said.

Do you want me to carry you? said Ron.

We'll get an ambulance, said Claire.

No! I said. You have to give him time.

Time for what? said Polly.

I don't know. Come on. Let's go to the hotel.

When we got to the Midland Hotel, it was in darkness like everywhere else. We asked the doorman what had happened. No one knows . . . there's no TV, no internet, the emergency services are at hospitals and railway stations. The trains are stranded on the tracks.

And silently I thought, this will give Victor the time he needs.

Ron and Claire were staying in a suite. Ron booked Polly and me a room each, waving away my offer of a credit card.

Get 'em a toothbrush and a bottle of brandy, will you? he said to the doorman.

I'll pray for us all, said Claire, which seemed almost sensible under the circumstances.

Polly and I took the stairs to our rooms.

Polly, I said, don't do anything just yet. Please. Talk to me in the morning. Just wait, will you?

Polly reached up and kissed me on the lips. A simple kiss. It didn't feel wrong. It felt like some kind of acknowledgement of whatever had happened tonight.

But what had happened tonight?

I didn't go to bed.

As soon as I heard her bathwater running, I left the hotel in the wartime darkness, and made my way towards the entrance to the tunnels.

The city was like a city under curfew. Empty. Dark. There was a guy in a doorway huddled in a sleeping bag.

What happened? I said.

Whole thing went black, he said. Just black.

Far away a siren tore through the streets.

When I got back to the tunnel entrance the outer gate was closed and locked. My heart leapt. That means Victor is out and clear!

I began to walk swiftly to his apartment. I was cold, soaked, bruised and exhausted, and it didn't matter.

His building was in darkness, of course. The main door had locked on Default at the outage. The doorman wasn't there. I went round the back and up the fire escape. We've done this before, he and I, sneaking in like teenagers having sex for the first time.

Is that what it felt like?

Maybe it did.

At the top of the fire escape there's a Parkour-style leap onto Victor's terrace. I leapt, not looking down at the black hole opening beneath me.

His sliding doors were unlocked. I went in. That familiar smell. His pomegranate candles.

Victor?

He never moves anything, so I found the matches and lit the candle. And another and another. The place looks like a shrine. Such an orderly man. He leaves no trace of himself.

But if he's left the tunnels, he'll soon be back.

I took a shower. I put on his nightshirt. I got into his bed and slept, waiting for daylight.

We are lucky, even the worst of us, because daylight comes.

Humanity is not a steady-state system.

Any butcher will sell you one.

Lamb or ox.

Human looks much the same.

About the size of a clenched fist. The body's circulatory pump. The heart inclines to the left – two thirds of its mass is on the left side. The heart is not dry; it sits inside a fluid-filled cavity. Nor is it single. There are four chambers, the right and left atriums and the right and left ventricles. The atria are bloody chambers, fastened to the veins that bring blood to the heart. The ventricles, connected to the arteries, carry the blood away from the heart. The right-side chambers are smaller than those on the left. At any given time the chambers of the heart may be found in one of two states: systole, when the cardiac-muscle tissue contracts to push blood out of the chambers, or diastole, when the cardiac muscles relax to let blood into the chambers. This process gives us the numbers we need to take our blood pressure. In my case, 110 (systole) over 65 (diastole).

The heart begins to beat at day twenty-two in the womb. It never stops.

Until it does.

*

Victor has been gone eight days now.

I'm wearing his jacket. I have used up the milk in the fridge. I started to rummage for the accumulations of a life. There were none. He lives like he's in someone else's home, except it's his own – although when Polly started searching, she found that the apartment belongs to a company registered in Switzerland. No further information has been forthcoming.

I went along to HR at the university. I don't exist as far as they are concerned. Not a relative. Not a partner. I am not named on his form: Who To Contact In The Event Of An Emergency. I asked, Who is? They couldn't say; only that it is a company in Geneva.

Dr Stein has taken leave.

Leave of what? His senses?

People don't just disappear.

But you see, in the world we live in, he hasn't disappeared; his bills are settled. The correct forms have been filled in. By whom?

In any case, the massive outage in Manchester was simultaneous with a city-wide IT meltdown. Millions of gigabytes of data wiped. Including, says Polly, Victor's records.

His phone is dead.

A couple of weeks later, Polly managed to get access to the tunnels. She took me with her. It was a different entrance, not the one we had used. I asked about that one. No such way in, said our guide. Not since the 1950s, anyway. Blocked off.

We went down like visitors to an underworld we used to know.

There was the pub where we had told our stories. But everything was as it should have been. No overturned tables or flooded floors. The board games and cards were neatly stacked on the shelves. The photo of Winston Churchill had new glass. I know it was new glass. I ran my finger over it. No dust.

The giant generators, Jane and Marilyn, were clean and silent.

And everything else had gone too. The concrete rooms were empty. No jumping spiders. No lurching hands. No busy bots slicing brains, no heads in jars, no computers. Only the swinging overhead strip lights and the boom boom of the River Irwell.

As we were leaving, the lights going out behind us as our irritable guide flicked off the Bakelite switches, I kicked something underfoot. I bent down and closed my hand around it. I could feel what it was; he took it off when he went to work on the head.

Victor's signet ring.

I went back to his apartment once more. I had a few clothes to collect. The key didn't work in the lock so I rang the bell. A hostile woman answered. She was the new tenant. What did I want? I explained about my clothes. She told me to contact the agent and slammed the door in my face.

Pity . . . I liked that T-shirt.

Down the stairs. Down the stairs. Down the stairs. The door closes for the last time.

Here I am. Anonymous, unnoticed, walking through the streets, and I am present and invisible. The riot in my head is unseen. What I am thinking, what I am feeling, are private Bedlams of my own. I manage my own madness just as you do. And if my heart is broken it keeps beating. That is the strangeness of life.

Message from Polly: *Do you want dinner tonight?*

Maybe I do.

What is your substance, whereof are you made,
That millions of strange shadows on you tend?

Any butcher will sell you one.

I have bought them often enough when we had little money. The thing most prized in humans is the cheapest meat:

The heart.

As Shelley burned on that brittle mound of dried wood, his chest fell open, and our friend Trelawny snatched his heart from the funeral pyre.

In India the widow is expected to ascend the funeral pyre to follow her husband to his end. Her life is over.

But it is not. We are stubborn. We survive. Grief alone does not kill us.

I could be free . . . If I could pluck out the memory of him from my heart as easily as his heart was plucked from the fire, I could be free.

I discover that grief means living with someone who is no longer there.

The Buddhists believe that our returning spirit may inhabit any form it chooses. Is that him? Mistletoe on the winter oak. Is that him? Swooping above me in the body of a bird. I could wear him on my finger in the ring he gave me. If I rub it, will he appear again in human form?

There is a feral cat that comes here most days . . . such wild, nocturnal eyes.

I have taken some of the ashes of his heart and wrapped them up with a lock of his hair and a few letters to me.

The remains of the remains. It is absurd that what we are vanished without trace. Ada Lovelace said to me last week that if we could re-present ourselves in a language that the Analytical Engine could read, then it could read us.

Read us back to life? I said.

Why not? she said.

He would enjoy that; to be read back to life. Imagine it; his poems in my pocket, and him too. I feed the punch-card into the machine and what comes out is Shelley.

Mary! he says.

(Victor! Is that you?)

I turn round. In the crowd. Over there. Is that him?

Shall we begin again?

The human dream.

A NOTE FROM THE AUTHOR

This story is an invention that sits inside another invention – reality itself. Alcor is a real place. So is Manchester. So was Bedlam. The tunnels under Manchester are there – but not quite as I have described them. Some characters in this story existed, or still do. Others are fictions. None of the conversations took place in the way that they appear here – or perhaps at all. I hope I have caused no offence to the living or to the dead. This is a story.

ACKNOWLEDGEMENTS

Thank you to everyone who has worked with me on this book at Jonathan Cape and VINTAGE, especially Rachel Cugnoni, Ana Fletcher, Bethan Jones and Laura Evans. To Susie Orbach, who believes in the biological human more than I do. And to my agent and friend, Caroline Michel.

This book is dedicated to my godchildren, Ellie and Cal Shearer, who will work to make the future they want to see.